ALSO BY KAT & STONE BASTION

No Weddings Series

No Weddings · One Funeral

Two Bar Mitzvahs · Three Christmases

For Valentine's

Unbreakable Series

Heartbreaker · Rule Breaker · Lawbreaker

Forthcoming: *Ball Breaker · Icebreaker*

Highland Legends Series

Forged in Dreams and Magick

Bound by Wish and Mistletoe

Born of Mist and Legend

Found in Flame and Moonlight

THE TRAVELER: Initiate Years

Veil of Realms · Secrets of Alexandria · Panther Rising

Stones of Power · Highland Magick

Half-Baked Holidays

Half-baked Holidays:

A Romantic Comedy Holiday Collection

"The No Weddings series has a group of such amazing characters; you can't help but relate to them and feel the emotion in every situation they encounter. It has been a long time since a story has made me feel that way let alone an entire series!"

— *UNDER THE COVERS BOOK BLOG*

"The story of Cade & Hannah's relationship is realistic, heart-warming, and filled with real-world connections that shook me in a way that few titles I've read this year have managed...I have loved every minute of the No Weddings series."

— *THAT'S WHAT I'M TALKING ABOUT*

Heartbreaker

"This book has definitely earned its five stars and I am just floored right now. The passion is explosive, the story itself is beautiful, and the emotions are so real my heart is ready to burst. Beautiful book. Absolutely breathtaking."

— *ONE PAGE AT A TIME*

"Heartrending, passionate, and captivating! *Heartbreaker* is a riveting page-turner that will leave you breathless with raw emotions, and the need to hold tight to the ones you love!"

— *BENEATH THE COVERS BLOG*

"This book is all about flawless writing, exemplary storytelling, f*#king insane character development. The right dose of sexy hotness..."

— *LOVE N. BOOKS*

"The Bastions are at it again with this beautiful and heartbreaking story. You will absolutely fall in love with Kiki and Darren's love."

— *UNDER THE COVERS BOOK BLOG*

"*Heartbreaker* is a phenomenal story."

— *THAT'S WHAT I'M TALKING ABOUT*

"I loved it...wonderfully compelling, a story that touched my heart in so many ways and characters I will remember for a long time to come."

— *GIRL WHO READS*

AWARDS & PRAISE FOR KAT BASTION

Forged in Dreams and Magick

First Place – Unpublished Beacon Award
Best Paranormal Romance

First Place – Hold Me, Thrill Me Award
Best Paranormal Romance

Chosen by FreshFiction.com as their
Fresh Pick for October 22, 2013

"A beautifully woven tale about love, choices, courage and destiny, *Forged in Dreams and Magick* is one of the best time-traveling novels. Fans of Gabaldon's *Outlander* will love it."

— *BOOKISH TEMPTATIONS*

"I was gripping my iPad like a crazy woman and fanning myself from the smoldering romance. Lawdy!"

— *THE FLIRTY READER*

"Bastion's debut is pure perfection, a combination of romance, magic, emotion, adventure and surprising twists and turns. This is a truly unique romance that should not be missed!"

"HOLY HELL!!! I am so... um... wow! FABULOUS-NESS. *Forged in Dreams and Magick* definitely makes my BEST OF list for 2013..."

"A story guaranteed to enthrall with lushly detailed travels into times long gone by. Woven with love, passion, magic and legend, the story had me hooked from the very first chapter."

"Kat Bastion's wonderful debut brings a new voice to the fore. Her voice is strong and unhesitating, very human and real, sometimes young and delicious in her treatment of intimacy and relationship development."

"OMG, Bastion hits all cylinders in this supernatural tale. The layers in the book were fascinating, and I devoured the fun, adventuresome read."

Bound by Wish and Mistletoe

"I LOVED it! *Bound by Wish and Mistletoe* is, to my mind, a perfect entry in the historical / paranormal fiction genre and has quite a bit to offer."

"Kat Bastion has done it again! ... Excellent holiday novella, perfect for a cup of cocoa and snuggling under a blanket in front of the fireplace this holiday season."

"Move over, Julia Quinn and Sabrina Jeffries! Kat Bastion is an absolutely gifted author and deserves to be recognized for her talent."

FOR VALENTINE'S

FOR VALENTINE'S

KAT & STONE BASTION

Cover and layout copyright © 2021 Kat Bastion

Cover art copyright © Perfectfortune/Depositphotos

ISBN: 9780692023822

❀ Created with Vellum

To all who spread love with laughter...

1. WEDDED BLISS

I woke with a charged jolt.

Or was I still dreaming? Sure as fuck felt like it: heart racing, body sweating, full breath just out of reach.

But then in the middle of the cold, pitch-black room, warmth suddenly covered me—smooth skin, tempting curves, endless territory of the best thing that existed to get lost in, plenty of therapy to cure what ailed me.

"You okay, babe?" Hannah asked.

Soft lips covered mine seconds later, cutting off my ability to reply. Didn't need to. She knew.

I sighed as my tense muscles eased under her touch. "Yeah. Just a bad dream."

Nightmare, actually. Didn't know the fuck why, but they kept coming. Right at the time I had everything I wanted, the only thing I needed—Hannah.

But the fact that we'd gotten married hadn't seemed to register down to my subconscious. Nope. Apparently some twisted issue had been buried deep into my psyche and still needed to be worked out.

One reason why the upcoming weekend was so important.

"Another nightmare?" Gentle kisses trailed along my jawline. "What are they about?"

Dark. Filled with anguish. Tormented images. Of my ex. But no way in hell would I tell Hannah that. Didn't want to give more thought to the mental clusterfuck than necessary. So I admitted all I could. "Shadows from behind, threatening me. Choking me." True fucking shit.

"What can I do to help?"

I closed my eyes. "Just love me."

A silky curtain of hair shifted across my cheek as she moved her slight weight onto me. Her faint tropical scent surrounded me. Puffs of warm breath fogged over my lips.

Neither of us could make out the other in the darkness, and yet, we saw everything.

She stretched her entire body like a lazy cat: arms reaching beyond my head, over my pillow, legs vibrating along mine before the bottoms of her feet dragged up my calves. Then in one smooth arching movement, she curved her hips, grinding down.

I groaned low, cock hardening.

Her upper body pressed heavier onto my chest as she wrapped her hands underneath my shoulders, tightening her hold on me. "I do. I love you, Cade Michaelson, with all my heart. I always will. Never doubt that."

To prove her claim, she began to love me—her body might've been the device, but her heart powered the engine. Every kiss held more heat, even in their gentleness. Her fingers pressed harder as she rubbed them down my arms, then back up over my shoulders.

Not sure exactly when the switch flipped. But it

happened. Our tenderness flowed into what it often did: something carnal.

Hard fingernails raked across my chest as her sudden gasp sounded out. Hot breath fanned over my cheek. Her hips ground down harder as a low groan from her throat dragged into one of those decadent purrs I loved so much.

And she hadn't even taken me inside her body yet.

A shudder tremored through her as I ran my hands over her shaking thighs. After sliding over the flare of her hips, I gripped her sexy ass. Not hard, not taking control, but just enough to let her know I had her.

Teeth gently bit the skin over my jawbone on the side of my chin. "Bet I can give you better dreams," she whispered.

I groaned as she curved her pelvis and wet heat slid over me, coating my rigid length. "No doubt," I growled out between labored breaths.

Hers had reduced to short gasps followed by low moans. Anticipation had her riding the razor's edge of pleasure she loved to balance on. Dragging it out took her there faster and hotter, whether or not she was the one doing the teasing.

But this time she was in charge, taking care of me. And I let her. I needed every bit of the love she delivered.

Her body trembled harder, both from her arousal and her barely held restraint. She was there, hovering over at the brink, ready to fall.

She leaned forward, dragging her lips up my neck. A sudden gasp was followed by heavy, short breaths at my ear. Her body froze. We remained that way for long seconds as she reined in her body.

Teeth tugged at my earlobe. She inhaled again, then swallowed hard. "You ready?"

I choked out a laugh. "*Fuck* yes."

Warm, wet pressure surrounded the tip of my cock, and I pinched my eyes shut. My mouth fell open on a quiet gasp at the incredible pleasure.

A low whimper dragged from her throat as she lowered herself onto me, inch by slow inch. Her hands shifted to the front of my shoulders, then to my chest as she leveraged herself, pressing down, taking me all the way in.

My breaths grew ragged as I tried to control the fire shooting through me. I gripped her hips, forcing myself not to move. Or thrust.

Fuck, I wanted to arch up, pound into her. Take my pleasure...deliver hers.

Her hips rocked while she rode my cock, which was buried deep, rock hard and straining. Angling her pelvis, she slowly arched back, then curved forward, rubbing her clit against me. A purr vibrated out from her throat, and she whimpered softly. Short breaths and a quivering inhale came seconds before her low, long moan.

Her body suddenly went rigid. Then she screamed, digging her nails into my chest.

Fuck restraint. I tightened my hold on her hips, lifted, then pounded deep, gravity aiding my cause.

She was lost in a powerful orgasm that kept coming, her inner muscles gripping me hard and hot. But with her palms planted firmly, she took over, rising up, then slamming down.

Ache fired up through my balls, blazing over nerve endings until I roared from the intense pressure release, my rapid pulses firing deep inside her. Time seemed to stand still, breath escaping me. All that existed was blinding pleasure. Hers. Mine. *Heaven.*

In slow motion, our movements began to still. Shorter gasps of air lengthened into lungfuls.

She collapsed onto me, limp.

Breathing hard, I wrapped my arms around her. No thoughts existed, only a euphoric haze. The incredible aftermath we had never ceased to amaze me. Visceral, it cut me to the bone every time. Had to be the emotional connection —deeper than any other.

Her breaths finally slowed, and she shifted, nestling her cheek just below my collarbone. She pressed a soft kiss to my neck before movement spread out in a small tug, like she'd smiled. Then her hips wriggled.

I groaned. Semihard, my body warred with needing a timeout and wanting another round. "Tease," I growled.

"How was that?" she asked.

"Which? Your incredible fuck or you offering me more?"

A soft puff of air hit my neck. "Both."

"You tell me. Felt fucking amazing from my side."

"Ditto. I love riding you."

I rubbed my thumb along the ridge of her hipbone. "You do it spectacularly."

"And the bad dream?"

I exhaled a slow breath, closing my eyes, luckiest bastard on Earth to be loved by Hannah. "Long forgotten."

2. LIFE'S ABOUT THE ADVENTURE

"It has good bones." I blinked hard, then scrubbed a hand over my face, trying to wake the fuck up. Had to be after 5:00 p.m., but my ass had dragged through the day like a malnourished zombie. Damned bad dreams. They kept fucking with me enjoying my great reality.

My three sisters milled about, scanning over every square inch of the place for its possibilities. "Who cares about rickety old bones? Look at this view." Kendall took a few more steps, then rested a hand on the carved stone railing.

Kiki tapped a finger on her chin, staring up at the elaborate crown molding. "We wouldn't want to do too much to the place. Better to bring it back to its former glory."

"What do you think?" Kristen asked.

Good fortune had made this rare historical gem available. Our on-site meeting was to discuss the feasibility of taking the property and our event-planning business to the next level.

I shrugged, noncommittal about the whole thing–only

way I could stay objective when the topic involved pouring our own dollars and futures into the project. "The potential is there. The foot traffic alone and historical draw warrants a hard look."

Kiki stepped into my line of sight, eyebrows raised. Then she pointed, repeating Kendall, as if I hadn't heard. "Look at the view."

I did. And it was spectacular: dark hair, bright smile, hopeful eyes.

Of course, they hadn't meant Hannah. But when she was in the vicinity, all I saw was her. The rest of the world? Scenery.

Hannah stood with her back to us, overlooking the Schuylkill River. The waterfall rushed down its wide step in the distance, but she stared beyond it, up toward the sky. As I approached her from behind, she glanced over her shoulder with a widening smile.

I gave her a gentle hug, wrapping my arms around her waist and resting my hands just under her ribs. "What do you think, Mrs. Michaelson?" Only opinion I cared about.

Leaning back against my chest, she let out a lazy sigh. Then she nodded her chin in the direction of where she'd been looking. "That's our park over there."

"Sure is," I whispered, kissing her ear. "We've had some great memories here. Impromptu picnics..."

"Ginormous snapdragon bouquets..."

Yeah. That had been quite the feat of engineering. But desperate men in love pulled off miracles. "Puppy test-drive outings..."

She laughed at the mention of Ava as a tiny pup. I snorted on a headshake, recalling me scraping up dog shit from the sidewalk. But I grinned, loving every moment of the times we'd had. And I planned to have plenty more.

My sisters joined us at the railing, and Kristen turned toward me. "Well, do you want me to work up a proposal for Invitation Only's event portion? Think it might work for you and Hannah?"

Down to the nuts-and-bolts analysis, I gave a short nod. "Yeah. But we don't want to keep the current restaurant. Hannah and I talked about doing something different to breathe more life into the place."

Hannah wrapped an arm around me as she fully faced them. "What do you guys think about an upscale wine bar that serves desserts specifically made to complement the wines?"

Kiki grinned. "I love it! Like...there could be wine and dessert flights."

Kendall typed a note into her phone. "Great idea. Maybe even offer hors d'oeuvre samplers, like we'd serve at the events."

I gave a short nod. "Exactly. The wine bar can be open on a regular basis. We'd have to figure out the hours and days. But if we bring our brand of uniqueness to the place, give customers a taste with what we create for the wine bar, some will be interested in having Invitation Only do their events, here or elsewhere."

Silence followed as everyone mulled over the concept.

Kristen spoke first. "We should do weddings."

I choked out a dry laugh. "Very funny." But when I caught her expression, and all of their dead-serious looks, I shook my head. Hannah hadn't flinched, but I glanced down to find her blinking and wide-eyed, just as surprised as I was by the ambush. Damn good thing.

I glared at Kristen, architect of this coup. "*Fuck* no. No weddings."

The hard determination in her gaze never wavered. "I'm

nixing that rule. Your aversion to it is a nonissue. Besides, we'd made that agreement long ago when you couldn't keep your hands off of bridesmaids."

And when I'd harbored serious commitment issues of my own. But all that had changed with Hannah. Still, women didn't get it. Men had an ingrained aversion to froufrou and fuss.

Kendall waved a dismissive hand at me. "You two got married on the water."

Kiki's gaze turned fierce, like she was ready to do battle to win me over. "Kendall's right. So is Kristen. You can't shoot this down over a dumb technicality." Her eyes narrowed. "You pulled out all the stops when you wanted to marry Hannah, and we helped you do it. Now we have a chance to make that happen for other couples in love. What say you?"

Hard to argue logic. And the rule had become obsolete where I was concerned. Hannah had done that for me.

When I glanced down at Hannah, she looked up at me with pleading puppy-dog eyes. Yeah, I was a goner. I sighed in defeat. "I say it's a great idea."

Screams nearly pierced my eardrums. If that didn't kill me, the crushing group hug just might. I laughed and hugged my sisters and Hannah back. "Do not make me regret signing on for this, though. Kristen, you are completely in charge of Invitation Only. If you need our help, you've got it. But that business is your baby. Hannah and I have our own to run."

"Done," Kristen agreed without hesitation. Then we threw our hands into a huddle, counted to three, and broke on it with a "Michaelson Musketeers!" shout. Childhood. In a flash.

Then my adult brain started firing, blood pumping at the thought of being in business again—with Hannah. We would both officially leave the ranks of the unemployed. "I'll call the preservation trust office next week and set up a time to present a proposal. How many days will you need to work up your portion?"

Kristen stared over the water for a moment, then glanced back at me. "I can work on it over the weekend. Then we should meet to make sure yours and ours work synergistically."

I grinned, proud as hell of Kristen. She was a natural at running a business. "Hannah and I can meet with you on Tuesday, then schedule to present anytime Wednesday or after?"

Kiki began to walk toward the main building in the fading daylight. "We need to meet too. I've got design thoughts that I'll put on paper for you to include in the presentation. We'll keep the historical aspects, but there are lots of other things we can do to improve on what's here."

"Have at it," I agreed. "Whatever we can do to take the site to the next level? Include." When my best friend, Ben, and I had opened Loading Zone almost two years ago? Kiki had transformed the rundown warehouse into a widely acclaimed "industrial-grunge" bar. As far as design was concerned? Kiki had free reign.

Kendall tugged Kristen's arm. "I gotta go. I have a work function to get ready for."

Kiki joined them as they headed toward Kristen's SUV. Kristen glanced over her shoulder. "You guys good?"

I pulled the keys to the place from my pocket and jangled them out in front of me. "Yeah. We'll lock up and drop these back off."

Not sure how we were doing on time, I slid my hand into Hannah's, then tilted her wrist toward me. Her watch showed we had another twenty-five minutes before the park offices closed.

Hannah nestled closer into my side on another sigh.

The silence between us, right as it felt, was thick with emotion. I smiled and kissed the top of her head. "You like the place?"

Her voice came out just above a whisper. "I love it."

She turned in my arms. "It's a little bigger than a hot dog stand."

I tried not to laugh. "That it is, Maestro. But wine and desserts suit you better."

With a quick glance at the stone buildings, her expression fell. "I didn't imagine we'd be *taking over* a business. Somehow I thought we'd build one of our own."

"We will make this our own. But it's only our first venture. We've got the rest of our lives to create whatever we want."

Her eyes softened as her gaze fell to my lips. "I like that thought."

Pulling her closer, I smirked. "What thought is that? Your hungry expression makes me think work is the last thing on your mind." The deep pink blush on her cheeks gave away just how naughty her thoughts had gone. "Really? We're talking about business and in two seconds flat you want to jump me?"

She broke away with a gentle shove to my chest. "It's your fault. Your touching me does it."

I held my hands up, doing my best to impersonate innocence. "I did nothing. But just so we're clear: For us to work together, there's a hands-off policy?"

Her mouth broke into a wide grin. Then her teeth

tugged on that sexy lower lip of hers as she took a few steps backward. "I'm not making any rules. You'll only break them."

True. I tilted my head down, gaze never leaving hers, and stalked forward, matching her slow retreat step for step. Then my attention scanned downward. "What are those things over your legs? You've never worn them before. Not sure I approve." They hid all her tempting olive skin from me.

She clutched her purple scarf and the lapels of her knee-length black coat as she opened her arms wide. "They're knit tights. To keep my legs warm. There are other things in this world meant to go under my skirts besides petticoats."

"Unthinkable." I smirked. "But now all I *can* think about is what's under those knit tights."

She stretched her arms behind her, which pulled the material of her dress taut over her breasts. Her nipples had hardened. A fact my eyes caught even in the dim light—a Cade Michaelson superpower.

I heaved in a breath. "*I* am meant to go under your skirt. The *most important* thing."

Mischief glittered in her eyes a split second before she made a run for it in the opposite direction. I let her think she could escape, but her feeble attempt at speed gave her away. She wanted to get caught.

After an easy jog, I captured her with a gentle colliding hug, swept her into my arms, and backed her against the stone railing before sitting her onto its wide surface. Her soft laughter rang out as I nudged her legs open and stepped between them.

Heart racing from more than the chase, I bent down and ran my lips a hairsbreadth from her neck beginning at her collarbone and ending just below her ear with a slow exhale. She shivered and wrapped her arms around my shoulders.

I nipped her earlobe with my teeth, growling low. "The things I am going to do to you under that skirt. *Filthy-as-fuck* things that will have you begging for more."

Her voice was a breathless whisper. "Oh, like what?"

"You know I don't give itineraries." I slid my hands up under the soft fabric of her short dress. The waistband of the tights gave way to my exploration.

The moment my fingers slid along warm skin, she gasped and gripped my biceps. "Your hands are freezing."

"I'm pretty sure they won't be much longer." When I skimmed lower, I blinked and pulled back. "You're not wearing a thong."

She gave me a slow headshake. "I usually go commando with tights."

"*Fuck.* I'm liking tights more and more." I gripped the sexy globes of her ass, and she groaned, leaning toward me.

She let out a measured breath. "We can't have sex right here."

"Oh, we *can*. It's entirely possible and definitely feasible." I'd completely blocked her with my body. Would it be risky in this very public place? Yeah. Would it be asinine to do it, knowing we sought to run a potential business here? Absolutely.

I pulled her closer. Her tight-covered legs dangled around my thighs. But my thoughts were stuck on the juncture of her legs where she pressed against the groin of my jeans—where my cock had hardened to such a degree, the ache had grown nearly unbearable.

She didn't stop me. In the public place, where no one was currently nearby, but the threat of discovery existed, she trusted me, laid herself wide open and vulnerable in my care.

I reluctantly dragged my hands away from her pert little ass, then righted her dress. On a slow inhale, I pulled her coat together, buttoning her halfway up, then tied her scarf into a loose knot under her neck. The breeze blew her dark hair across her face until I gently brushed it back over her cheek and tucked it behind her ear.

She had the nerve to give me a smirk.

I arched a brow. "Behave. I'm doing the protective gentleman thing here. But you've gotten me horny as fuck right now. My resolve could turn on a dime."

Doing her best not to smile, she pressed her lips together and gave me a short nod.

I shook my head on a laugh and helped her down. The amusement still dancing in her eyes did not go unnoticed. "You don't fool me for a second. I know you're scheming about how to snap the thread on my control."

She clasped both of her hands around one of mine, tugging us toward her car. "I'm not going to push any buttons. I was merely thinking you've found a great hand warmer."

I barked out a laugh. "Your ass? See..." —I wrapped an arm around her shoulder, pulling her against my side— "you have the best ideas when we get naughty."

On a last glance back at the historic property, I saw what they had all seen: potential. The possibility of transforming an already great business into something extraordinary fired me up.

And with this weekend kicking off a new era for Hannah and me, I looked forward to putting all of our past— including subconscious fears—behind us. So we could forge a brighter future.

MINUTES LATER, Hannah and I dropped the keys off at the nearly deserted park trust office. Then after negotiating through Thursday night rush hour traffic, we finally hit the interstate.

"Why again are we leaving tonight?" She reached over the gearshift and threaded her hand into mine.

"Because I've planned a detailed, full schedule for the weekend."

"Of which, you're not sharing a thing with me."

I fought a smile. "Nope."

She laughed. "Did you just pop your *p*?"

"Yep." Popped that one too. Oh yeah, I was a happy fucker. Girl by my side. On our way to rewrite a holiday into a *wonderful* thing I dream about? Even better.

Actually, Valentine's itself wasn't the issue. It was the train-wrecked proposal that had happened on the specific calendar day three years ago: when I'd gotten my heart crushed with a laughing turndown, then my ex revealed she'd been cheating on me all along. So, yeah. The hearts and flowers thing needed a total redo.

Hannah shook the ice in her nearly empty iced green tea, then loudly sucked up the last of the liquid through the straw. "Well, we're heading north. So I know it's not Florida."

I glanced at her with a grin. "See? Who needs the road map? You can enjoy the scenery and read the signs along the way."

She stuck her tongue out at me. Fucking adorable.

Inside that sexy-as-fuck exterior, pulled straight from my fantasies, was a vulnerable girl who'd also had her heart shattered. An asshole groom had been a no-show to their wedding. Which was a great thing. She'd been meant for me.

And last Valentine's had been the first time either of us had trusted after that. In fact, on that fateful night, we'd turned to one another. Not in any major leap, but a start. That night, Valentine's Day one year ago, had been a major event for us as a couple. So in a way, the upcoming weekend was our anniversary trip.

I imprinted that monumental factoid into my brain, hopefully branding it firmly into my subconscious. *Take* that *you fucking nightmares.*

A loud sound garbled out, then she giggled.

"Was that your stomach?" I glanced at her.

"Yeah. How long before we get to wherever we're going?"

I frowned. "Not for several hours. I should've taken us to dinner first." In my excitement to get out of town, I'd forgotten to feed us. *Nice boneheaded move, Cade.*

"Do we have time for a detour?" She opened the glove box, then pulled out a folded map and mini Maglite flashlight.

"Sure." The schedule wasn't that tight. If we hit our destination sometime tonight and got a great night's sleep, we'd have plenty of time to squeeze it all in. "What about in Willow Creek? I think I ate at a decent restaurant there years ago."

Massive amounts of crinkling followed as she origami'd that map into five different configurations while juggling the flashlight. Once she had folded back everything but the section she wanted to focus on, she popped the Maglite into her mouth.

Fuck if my mind didn't gutter that picture, fantasizing about her luscious lips wrapped around something else. Something definitely wider in girth.

"Okay. Here." She pointed at the map, as if I could see it.

I waited as she pulled it closer to her face, narrowing her eyes.

"Hmmm. Doesn't look like there's a turnoff there. We have to get off two exits before, then work our way through side streets. You up for the adventure?"

"With you?" I glanced at her. "I'm up for anything."

3. UNEXPECTED DETOUR

The outside temps dipped lower, causing our breaths to steam the windows. I glanced at the dashboard, then turned on the defroster. Nighttime lows dropping into the midtwenties were normal for this time in February, but we'd been experiencing a long-lasting warm front for weeks. Last night, however, had brought an unexpected snowfall and today had been colder than forecasted.

"There! That's the turnoff we need to take." She pointed to the road sign.

I changed lanes, merging onto the exit ramp, then slowed to a stop at the four-way intersection. After she fumbled with the map again, I turned left at her direction. About an eighth of a mile later, we turned onto a side road, resuming north.

The posted speed limit was 40. But with limited night-time visibility and the unfamiliar route, I kept to a safer 30.

Tall trees towered over either side of a winding country road. Every now and then, a dirt road appeared on the left or right, marked by a cluster of mailboxes, but then it was nothing but forest-lined corridor again.

"You positive about those directions?" A good ten minutes had gone by. I wasn't sure I remembered any of this. Seemed like we were driving deeper into the middle of a very desolate nowhere.

An S-curve sign gave us warning seconds before the gentle curve appeared ahead, flanked by a low, plowed snowbank. The road meandered left, and I turned the wheel. The car? Ignored the wheel. And plowed us straight toward the snowbank. Brakes? Ignored me as well.

"Hold on!" Everything happened in a blur. At the last second, I flung an iron arm out in front of Hannah's chest, bracing her for a jarring impact. The classic Mustang had no airbags. Or headrests. We lurched forward, then jolted backward and I shot my hand behind her neck, trying to protect her from whiplash. A loud *bang!* echoed and I tensed. But nothing more happened. The lap belts had prevented us from slamming into the dashboard. Barely.

She'd already been prepared and had braced herself. Thank fuck we'd been coasting level at about 30 mph and I'd slowed a bit approaching the darkened curve.

"You okay? Anything hurt?" What if she'd slammed a kneecap or her neck had been injured after all?

"I'm good." She nodded, eyes wide.

I unbuckled my lap belt and twisted in my seat, looking back at the road as I tried to process what had happened. "Black ice." *Tall trees, shadowed roadway, freezing nights... that'll do it.*

Twisting back around, I stared at the low snowbank we'd plowed into. The front end had sunk in a good couple of feet deep. I shifted the car into reverse, then gave the gas pedal a little pressure. The engine revved, but we didn't move. Not even an inch.

"Bear with me, while I try a few things." Rocking. Filed

somewhere in my memory, I checked off the list of things to do when stuck in mud or snow. In order to rock the car, we had to get some kind of motion. And since reverse hadn't done jack shit, I put the car in gear. It felt counterintuitive to send the car deeper into the snow, but it was worth a shot. I gave the car gas again.

Nothing.

Which meant we weren't getting any traction.

Fuck. I wished my roommate, Mase, hadn't needed the Jeep this weekend. We'd be back on the road by now. My gut also wrenched, thinking we'd possibly damaged Hannah's pristine Josephine, the '67 Mustang Fastback she inherited from her Granpop.

"I need to get out, babe." I grabbed my coat and gloves from the backseat. "Know off the top of your head what kind of emergency gear you have?"

She furrowed her brow. "A spare tire, a tire iron, and flares, I think."

I nodded, then prayed for more as I got out of the car and put on my gloves and coat while heading to her trunk.

Turned out, she had a few more things: jumper cables, silver emergency blanket folded into a small square, a multi-purpose tool, and a section of burlap underneath it all. That might work.

After moving aside the other items, I pulled out the long piece of burlap. I snorted, thinking of all the times Hannah and I had teased about lingerie being burlap. Yeah, well, I was sure as fuck glad she or her Granpop valued *actual* burlap.

Realizing I'd need two pieces, I grabbed the multipur-pose tool, rotated out a knife, and sliced through the mate-rial until I had two similarly sized pieces. I pocketed the tool. Then I grabbed the tire iron, squatted down, and did my best to dig snow out from under the back tires. Once a decent amount of each tire's underside had been exposed, I shoved the burlap as far beneath it as possible.

"You sure you don't need any help? I'm feeling useless in here." Hannah leaned out the now-open driver's window.

"No. You stay warm. That's being plenty useful." I stood and dusted wet snow off my gloves, surveying my work. "Besides, I'm done." I opened the driver's door, then slid onto the seat while Hannah moved back onto hers. I shut the door to keep the fast-blowing heat inside the car. "Let's see what that does." I shifted into reverse, then gave it some gas.

Fuck. Absolutely nothing.

I tried the whole rocking bit again. Nothing.

"We're definitely stuck." I shifted the car into first and cut the engine. No sense in wasting gas. I pulled my phone out of my coat pocket. "I've got roadside assistance. Not sure how long it'll take them to get here. Wherever 'here' is."

Hannah pulled out her trusty map with more crinkling.

I scrolled through my contacts, found the AAA roadside assistance entry, and clicked on it. The call didn't go through. I tried again. Nothing. Seemed to be the theme for the night.

"Reception is shit out here." I held up my cell phone toward the roof of the car, trying to get it to show anything other than "no service." No luck. Then I felt like a dumbass. Really? Like twelve more inches in altitude yields more reception?

I opened the car door again. "I'm going up to the rise I remember seeing. Maybe I can get a better signal."

Unreal. *Figures.* The one weekend I had a jam-packed schedule, down to the hours in between where we'd have time to ourselves, Mother Nature had to fuck things up.

I got to the top of the gentle rise. With no streetlights and no moon, I couldn't see a thing. There could've been a farmhouse on either side without its lights on, and I wouldn't have a clue. My phone, however, knew at least a cell phone tower had to be out there, because the reception strength increased from nothing to two bars. Doable for a phone call. I hoped.

Apparently my wish was granted: the call went through. They were able to guide me through getting a GPS coordinate on one of my phone apps, then I was informed that the nearest service provider would be dispatched out to our location.

"How far away is Fen's Garage?" I asked.

"My system shows twenty-seven miles away, sir," the service agent replied. "But we can't guarantee we'll be able to reach them right away. They have a required response time to be en route within thirty minutes of our call."

"I'll hold while you try." Yeah. Wasn't leaving that to chance. I'd had enough surprises for one night.

"Very well, sir. Please hold."

Hold I did. Standing on a dark stretch of road in the middle of nowhere with my girl in a car that we'd stranded, I hoped for a light at the end of the tunnel.

"Sir?"

"Yeah, I'm here."

"We were able to reach him. He said he will leave in about twenty minutes. My calculation shows he'll reach you around 8:30 p.m."

I pulled my phone back to check the time. Just under an hour and a half. "Thank you. We'll be waiting." I gave a smartass grin, even though she couldn't see it—wasn't directed at her, just the universe in general.

When I returned back to the car, Hannah had bundled

herself underneath her coat. Her eyes peeked out from over the top of the black wool collar at me.

I scowled and removed my coat and gloves before tossing them onto the backseat. After I got in and closed the door, I turned the engine back on and turned the heat up to full blast. "No way am I letting you freeze in here. It'll be about ninety minutes before the cavalry arrives."

She nodded, then stared at the dash with drawn brows. "Will we have enough gas?"

I stared at the gauge, double-checking the needle. Her Mustang was a beauty, but it was a serious gas guzzler. "Should be. We're at over three-quarters of a tank. I'll top it off as soon as we get going again."

She leaned against me, dropping her head to the side to rest on my shoulder. Her hand spread out over my chest until it rested over my heart.

I wrapped a hand around her shoulders, holding her close, as I pressed a kiss to the top of her head. As frustrating as it was to be helplessly stranded, there was no other person in the world I'd rather be stuck with than her.

She hummed low, turning her head a little as she burrowed closer. "It's so quiet here. It's kind of nice. Like we're parking."

I coughed out a laugh. "Parking, as in making out?"

When she lifted her head to look at me, a smile brightened her face. "Sure. We're confined in a car for over an hour until we're rescued. Can you think of anything else you'd rather do while we wait?"

I dropped a deadpan look at her. "Rhetorical question."

All the amusement vanished from her eyes. Instead, she held my gaze for a beat longer, then it drifted lower, settling on my mouth before she eased forward. Her lips grazed mine, barely making contact. Warm air from her slow exhale came seconds before firmer pressure followed in a soft kiss. Then another, as she opened her mouth to me, her tongue sliding across mine in invitation, before darting away. Teasing. Coaxing.

I groaned, pulling her closer.

Her hand drifted lower until it slid over the bulge in my jeans. Under her firm touch, it hardened further. She murmured, "Let's see about that answer."

Fuck yes. I kissed her back, harder, with more urgency.

I hadn't planned the crash, sure as hell would've avoided it if I could've, but my body was definitely glad she was on board with making the most of it.

4. SLIPPERY WHEN WET

W hen Hannah removed her hand from my crotch, cooler air seeped through the denim. Then her soft lips touched my earlobe seconds before hard teeth tugged on it. She reached over to the ignition and twisted the key, cutting the engine. "We won't need the heat for a while."

She was right. Windows? Already fogging.

The coat that she'd been huddling under only seconds ago, slid off of her as she shifted and knelt onto her seat. She bundled up the woolen material and tossed it into the back.

I'd planned this trip to be amazing, to get my troubling dreams in line with my incredible reality, and when we hit a little black-ice speed bump? Hannah grabbed the wheel...

My pulse kicked up at the desire in her darkened eyes. Needing to touch her, I slid a hand up her thigh.

My one-track mind screeched to a halt. "Uh..." Those knit-tight things still clung to her legs. "How do you propose we have sex with these things on?" I pinched the material away from her skin, then released it. The fabric was so soft, it didn't even snap against her skin properly. I scowled. "These come off."

She shook her head with an amused smile. "No. They're keeping me warm. Besides, who said you're getting any? We said 'making out.'"

I choked out a laugh. "For over an hour? You trying to kill me with blue balls?"

That luscious lip of hers disappeared behind her teeth as she negotiated carefully around the gearshift to attempt to straddle my lap. Not in any way resembling merely "making out." *Interesting.*

With my long legs, the seat was already adjusted back as far as possible. The steering wheel had nowhere to else go. But none of the cramped quarters made any difference to my determined woman. And she fit perfectly.

As her body settled over mine, all soft curves and temptation underneath the thin fabric of her dress, her lips brushed over my ear. "I promise you won't die. And there will be no blue balls."

Translation: sex.

She just wanted to play a little. Or a lot.

And I was the happiest fucking man on Earth to be her toy.

Her lips began a sensual path over my skin, trailing below my ear, dotting small kisses over my jawbone, until she reached my chin. Then she paused and swallowed hard.

Her chest heaved up and down, breasts pressing against me with every inhalation. Her fingers found their way into my hair, cradling the back of my head. Her intense gaze penetrated down deep, piercing my heart. "I love you, Cade Michaelson."

My lips curved into a smile. Before I had a chance to respond, her eyes drifted closed and she kissed me. Not hard and rough. Not urgent. She took her time, savoring each touch. Her tongue tasted mine, then her lips closed, denying me access. Until she sucked on my lower lip.

Unhurried, lazy and seductive, she backed up her words with her body. Our lips touching was the only skin to skin, but her body undulated over mine. Hips arched, then curved against me in slow rhythm. Her fingers tugged at my hair.

I groaned and closed my eyes, my cock hardening painfully behind my denim button fly. But I didn't pull the plug on her slow seduction. Nothing in the world would make me take control away from her.

After all, it wasn't every day that I blew it on keeping my girl safe on the road and she rewarded me with a pit stop into my fantasies. *Yeah. I've never had sex in a car. Go figure.*

On my quest in rewriting Valentine's Day, being stranded off course had suddenly become very appealing. I couldn't have planned it better.

She shifted, leaning back while she pulled her hands forward and worked them between us, but her lips never left mine. Our kisses intensified, more urgent. Between breaths, almost nonexistent low whimpers came from her throat. She tugged my T-shirt free from my jeans, then ran trembling fingers up my abs, skimmed them over my chest.

I ran my hands further up those knit-tight covered thighs, under her dress, over her hips, then gripped the curves of her ass.

Hot breath fogged over my lips on her low moan. Another torturous kiss followed as she ground her hips again. Then she adjusted once more, lifting until the buttons on my fly suddenly ripped open.

I swallowed hard, anticipation nearly killing me, until she pulled my cock free from the denim. I groaned, arching up into her hand as she wrapped her fingers around my shaft. She loosened her hold, moving her hand lower to the base, then gripped hard and pulled upward until her thumb traced along the underside of the tip.

Fuck. I sucked in a deep breath, exhaled through gritted teeth, and forced my thoughts to the only mundane thing my mind could lock on to with my lack-of-blood-flow brain, like if the car's grill sustained damage—all that kept me from shooting off right there in her hand.

With every ounce of restraint I had, I reined it in. Her hold loosened again, drifted down to the base, then slid back up, this time to rest all nine inches along my abdomen before dropping her body over the length.

I opened my eyes to find her staring down at me with a sexy fucking smirk on her face. She leaned back again, then angled her hips, riding my erection, with the only thing stopping me from shifting her hips and then penetrating her depths? An infuriating layer of knit fabric.

"Please tell me you're not planning to get us off by dry humping me with those things over your crotch."

Her hips continued to move, her breaths ragged, her eyelids drifting half shut. "I don't know. I'm pretty close to coming."

"Oh, no." I gripped her hips, immobilizing her. "I've never fucked in a car. There's no way we're driving away from here without officially doing it."

She held back laughter, amusement glittering in her eyes. "Really? Never once in all your playboy years? I *cannot* believe that."

I shook my head. "Nope. And if I had to pick a car and the woman? I'm glad it never happened until now."

Her expression softened. "Awww...I love that."

"Good." I gave her a hard nod, then lifted her a few

inches upward. "Glad we're on the same page. Can you hold yourself up for a minute or two?"

Her brows furrowed as she flexed her legs, rising higher. "I think so, why?"

I leaned an arm back between the seats, found my coat pocket, and dug out the multipurpose tool. Then I clicked on the dome light. After glancing down to verify there was a safe distance, I held my hand over the passenger seat, safely away from her, and flicked out the knife blade. "Hold still."

"What are you doing?" She stared at the sharp blade, alarm sparking in her widening eyes.

"Desperate man? Desperate measures." I assessed the task, glancing down between us. "Can you lift your dress out of the way?"

"Ummm...yeah, I think so." After a quick scan around us, she shifted her weight toward the car door, then lifted her dress with her other hand. Had she looked down, her view would've been blocked by the bunched fabric she'd gathered. Instead, her gaze held mine. Absolute trust radiated from those depths.

I plucked the knit fabric with my fingers, pulling it away from her waist. "Ready?"

She gave me a certain nod.

Knife in one hand, tights in the other, I pierced through the stretchy fabric with a tight flick of my wrist. Then I flipped the tool safely closed again, tossed it onto the back seat, grabbed both ends of the flimsy severed material, and pulled.

A ripping sound followed as the fabric dissolved under the strain. Down, down, until I could no longer see where it went. Unsatisfied, I slid my fingers along the waistband of the tights to her lower back, then trailed down along the seam until I found the edge of the ripped material. I gripped both sides into my fists and tugged outward, tearing the rest of it apart.

"Finally," I growled, then grabbed her ass and squeezed. My cock surged to life again, kicking up against her as she relaxed her thighs and dropped back down onto me.

Then, in what can only be described as a contortionist's feat, she shifted her weight and worked her legs up and around the bucket seat, her knees folding over my arms where they bent at the elbows. She reached and turned the light back off.

I arched a brow, smirking. "Planning on having any leverage with that position?"

The corners of her lips twitched as she leaned back a little, then settled down further. And the second she aligned herself perfectly, her wet heat riding the length of my hard cock, both of our eyes widened.

"Oh, yeah," she replied. Biting her lip, she curved her hips forward, then arched her back, gliding over me as she coated the entire length. "Holding the seatback is" —she exhaled a shaky breath, then gasped— "great leverage."

Who was I to argue? Building ache took over. My thoughts scattered. Every last ounce of mental energy went to keeping my breaths steady, holding back for her.

When she lifted, right as she passed over the tip, it kicked up and caught at her entrance. I thrust up—couldn't fucking help it. Then she dropped down. A delicious sound tore from her throat, a mix between a low groan and a plea-filled whimper.

Leaning back, she increased her leverage again, taking me deeper. She ground her hips against me, alternating between easing backward and pressing forward, curving and arching.

In the darkness, barely discernable, she rode me, wild

and shameless. Her eyes closed, breaths ragged, sounds: animalistic. And although a long-sleeve dress covered her body, in my mind, she was completely naked and I saw her clearly: gorgeous breasts swaying as she moved, lips parting on a sigh.

Pressure built as she buried me again and again into her hot, wet depths. "You're right," I bit out. "Angle...*fucking* incredible." I gripped her hips, not altering her course, but doing my best to hold on for her ride.

She cried out and her inner muscles clenched my cock. But only once. Her breaths dropped to shallow pants. She collapsed down onto me, cradling her body around mine. As her hot breath fogged over my ear, she continued to grind against me in slow, small movements.

"So close," she whispered.

I know. I barely held on, nerves sparking and fraying fast. I clenched my jaw, the tremendous ache growing painful. Blood roared in my ears.

Her breath caught and she froze. Her body shuddered.

Blazing heat surrounded my cock and I lost it. I gripped her hips hard and slammed upward.

She cried out, then screamed. Piercing echoes bounced off the metal and glass around us. But the sound was muffled by my deep growl. My release shot like lightning had fired from my balls straight into her. My whole body tensed, lungs frozen, as the sudden rush consumed me.

Gradually, our pulses slowed, hers, mine, as our muscles relaxed. I sucked air into my burning lungs, then dropped my face into the crook of her neck, gathering her close.

The sounds of her heavy breathing, her chest rising and falling, us clinging to each other in her car in the middle of nowhere, etched into my brain.

She didn't move. I didn't want to. My sleep-deprived

body began sinking down into the seat with the warm comfort of Hannah wrapped around me.

Cold!

I jolted awake, wide-eyed, heart racing a million beats a second. "What the—"

Reality crashed back into me as I looked down. Hannah was cleaning me with a small white cloth. The dome light in the car had been turned back on.

Her concerned expression changed to amusement as she fought a smile. "You passed out."

I scrubbed a hand over my face. "Holy shit. Really? For how long?"

She shrugged, then settled back into her seat, folding the cloth before pulling a fresh one out of a flat plastic pack. "Ten minutes, maybe. You started twitching, then breathing heavy. Then your face screwed up into a deep scowl."

Which explained the racing pulse. "Must've dropped right into a dream."

"A nightmare again?" The concern returned, her brows furrowing.

"Not sure. Probably." Nothing stuck in my memory. Just feeling helpless, running. Away from or toward something? I hadn't a clue.

"What time is it?" I buttoned up my fly as Hannah cleaned off her hands before she discarded the wipes into a plastic trash bag.

She pulled her phone out and clicked it on. "8:05 p.m."

"We've got about twenty-five more minutes, then."

A wicked grin curved her lips. "I can't stop thinking about the last hour."

"Oh? Did I snore?" I winked at her. Then I glanced down at my T-shirt. At least I hadn't drooled.

She plucked at the destroyed tights that hung loose around her thighs. "I can't believe you sliced these in two."

The deadpan look I shot her made her laugh.

"Okay. I guess I asked for it."

"Damn straight, you did. I was just sitting here, all innocent."

"Uh-huh..." She kicked off her shoes and dragged the severed pieces down and off each leg. "Not buying it. You would've lasted five innocent minutes before you made the first move. I merely beat you to it, taking charge."

"Fucking spectacularly too."

As she settled back, she let out a heavy sigh. "I'm totally commando." She squirmed her hips.

I pressed my lips together, doing my damnedest not to smile. "You cleaned up?"

She nodded.

"You were all excited about your commando status at the riverfront."

"Well, yeah, but that was with tights on. It wasn't *really* commando."

"So embrace your inner wildness. Break the rules. Bare-ass it in that dress like a queen."

She shook her head, then blushed a gorgeous shade of pink.

When her stomach rumbled again, she leaned back toward one of her packed bags, fished around in it, and pulled out a can of Blue Diamond Smokehouse Almonds.

I stared at the can in disbelief. "You mean you had food in the car the whole time?"

She shrugged and raised her brows with a half-apologetic expression.

I blew out a slow breath, a smirk twisting my lips, as I

watched her straighten her dress, doing her best to look innocent.

But her skin was still flushed.

And my body was still wrung out.

I ran my tongue across my teeth, gaze dropping down her body. "I'm *so* not sorry either."

———

"I'M NOT PEEING IN A CUP." Hannah narrowed her eyes at me.

"You're *not* going outside. Fucking nonnegotiable point. Too damned cold."

Had I gotten us into this mess? Yeah. But I wasn't going to risk her any further. We'd spent the last ten minutes debating the topic after she'd eaten nearly half a can of almonds. Another ten to fifteen minutes, and we'd have company. She'd insisted her bladder *would* burst. Imminently.

A heavy sigh sounded out beside me. She was irritated. And uncomfortable.

I glanced at her. When our gazes locked, her face softened and moisture glittered in her eyes.

Fuck. "I'm so sorry, babe." I lifted a hand to her face, rubbing her cheek with my thumb. "Pretend we're at home. We go in front of each other all the time." A memory flashed into my mind. "Even camping. Remember flashlight duty? Bear patrol?"

"Those times were different. You're inches away now." Her brow furrowed. "You'll hear it splatter into the cup."

"I'll turn the radio on."

She gave me a headshake. "No. I don't want you to waste the battery or the gas."

"I've got music on my phone." I started to pull it out.

A gentle hand pressed on my forearm, and I looked at her. Determination hardened her features.

"No. This is mortifying enough. I don't want to be reminded of it whenever a certain song plays." In midreach for the cup, she paused and pegged me with a hard glare. "Or you. You are *not* to remember a thing about this. Scrub it from your brain. All of it."

I held up a palm. "I swear. Nothing is about to happen here."

My brain, still fuzzy from being sex drugged, finally realized there was an easy solution to the problem. "How 'bout I just step out for a minute?"

"No." Her expression remained hardened. "I can do this. You stay."

She shifted forward. And I did the gentlemanly thing: turned away. I even cracked the window to let some fresh air in. Sounds of splattering followed seconds later.

As the tension in the car grew thicker, while she continued to pee in her cup, I decided conversation would be acceptable. "Good thing I cut those tights free."

Her laughter was choked off by a growl. "Do *not* make me laugh. It's hard enough for girls to aim."

"Right. No apparatus to direct."

And the peeing continued. "I'm warning you."

I raised my hands in surrender, glancing over my shoulder to make out the top of her head. "Hey. Just trying to distract you."

"Ummm...this cup is big enough, right?"

"Should be." Damn, I hoped so. "It's over thirty ounces. Just because you drank it all doesn't mean it'll all come out."

We remained silent for the seconds that followed until

the stream abruptly ended. I fought the urge to turn around and help. "You good?"

"Um, yeah."

When I finally turned around, she had the cup wedged between her two feet on the floorboard. The lid secured with a *snap!* before she lifted it up. She held it between her stiffened fingertips as if it was the plague. "Now what? I'm not confident this thing won't tip and spill."

I frowned. Yeah. We weren't topping off the most amazing car sex with...*that*. I got out of the car and leaned back in for the cup with an open hand.

She shook her head, pulling the cup out of reach. "What are you going to do?"

"Dump it on a snow bank." I waved my fingers toward me, beckoning her. "Give me the cup."

With hesitant movements, she finally gave up the goods. I walked out to the snow bank, leaned over the upper edge, carefully pulled the lid off, and poured the contents over the back side of the snowbank. As I walked back to the car, I scooped up snow, then dumped it out, effectively rinsing the cup, then put the lid back on.

When I returned and got back into the car, she had her plastic package of wipes out, one in use already as she cleaned her hands. I pointed toward the plastic trash bag with the empty cup. "Open the bag for me?"

She untied it and held it open while I ceremoniously dropped the cup inside. After our quick use of wipes, she tied off the bag again and stowed it behind her seat.

Her brows drew together. "I can't believe you poured a cup of my pee out there."

As I ran the wipe over my fingers, I shrugged. "You marked your territory. I was just the middleman. Had you gone pee outside, it would be there anyway."

"Just..."

"Stop stressing." On impulse, I lunged, twisted in my seat to pin her. Then I crushed my lips onto hers. Hard, insistent, I claimed her mouth until she surrendered her body and worries to the kiss.

When I pulled away, we were both breathless. I stared deep into her eyes, grateful for her, for this moment, for what we could do to each other with the slightest spark—make it ignite into flames.

I gave her a fierce look. "Nothing happened here but fucking incredible car sex."

She nodded with a dazed expression.

Fuck yeah. So far so good on the memory replacement front. Now if only I could get the great reality to penetrate my dreams.

5. RESCUE

"On top of a washing machine."

"Over the hood of a car," I added.

"The kitchen counter." Mischief glittered in Hannah's eyes as she tapped her phone again to keep the screen lit.

I cocked my head. "Haven't we done that before?"

"Nope. Not from beginning to end. You always get distracted with...*eating*...and then we end up on the floor."

"Okay. I'll give you that one." Fuck yeah, I would. "The bathtub."

"Isn't that kind of tight?"

I growled low, imagining how tight it would be. "And your argument would be?"

While we played our own road-trip game of places we wanted to fuck each other, headlights suddenly flashed in the darkness, and we startled upright. I immediately honked the horn and tapped the brake lights, hoping whoever approached wouldn't miss us.

Hannah turned fully around, kneeling as she clutched the top corners of her seatback. She leaned down, squinting at the blinding headlights that streamed in through the back window.

I stared at the side mirror, trying to make out the shape of the vehicle. A truck, diesel sound. Wide stance with a double set of tires maybe. I saw the overhead apparatus right as...

"Tow truck!" Hannah shouted.

I huffed out a relieved laugh. "Thank fuck."

A loud clang sounded, and I opened the car door.

Hannah never took her gaze away from the back window. "Do you think it's safe?" she whispered before I fully stepped out.

I glanced at the hulking form approaching our car. The guy could've been a linebacker with those shoulders. The way his headlights lit his bulldog stance from behind, he could've also made every horror flick's movie poster. The menacing shadow kept coming.

On a shrug, I gave Hannah a quick glance. "He's not carrying an ax. So we've got that going for us."

She narrowed her eyes at me.

I winked at her.

Was I an idiot? Fuck no. I slid the tire iron out from the floorboard behind my seat, just in case.

I kept my arm down and pointed toward the tires as he approached, using the weapon to illustrate rather than intimidate. "We're stuck and can't get traction enough to get out. Give us a hand?"

By the time he came within a few feet of me, I lowered the tire iron. With that boyish face, he had to be twenty tops. Concern furrowed his brow as he rubbed a hand over his mouth, staring at the car.

"You try rockin' it?"

I barely heard Hannah's soft laugh and swallowed my

smile. "Yeah, but the car won't budge. Might need the winch, I think the front end is lodged into the snow."

He gave a sharp nod. "I'll hook'er up. Got traction mats too. We'll gitcha folks out in no time." With a smile that made him look even younger, the guy thrust a hand forward. "Name's Fen."

"Fen?" I slipped my hand into a firm grip.

His smile widened. "Morgan Fendrick. But people just call me 'Fen.'"

"Good to meet you, Fen. I'm Cade." I glanced back to see a smiling Hannah waving out the driver's door. I grinned. "That's my wife, Hannah."

My wife. I grinned like a fucking idiot. Yeah, I would never get tired of saying those words.

In under ten minutes, Fen had set us free. Afterward, he inspected the front end to be sure we hadn't sustained any damage. Then a couple of signed papers and a hundred dollar tip had us on our way.

When I turned the car around to follow Fen back the way we'd both come, Hannah gripped the dashboard, twisting in her seat to stare at our abandoned trap of a snowbank. "We're not going to try to find the restaurant?"

I gave her an apologetic glance. "No, Fen said it closed two years ago."

Silence followed. And then Hannah and I both burst out laughing.

Hannah crossed her arms. "Well, I can cross that off my bucket list."

"What? Getting stranded on a desolate road?"

On a headshake, she settled back into her seat. "No. Having sex in a broken down car."

"It was not broken down, only stuck."

She shrugged. "Tomato, tomaaato."

"Me too."

"You too, what?"

"I can cross something off my bucket list," I replied.

"Oh, you had having sex in a broken down car too?"

"No." After we merged back onto a nearly empty highway, I shot her a deadpan look. "Being with my girl, stuck in a snowbank, after amazing sex in a '67 Mustang Fastback... *annnd* she peed in a cup."

She punched me in the shoulder. Hard. "You were never supposed to mention that."

"No," I countered. "I promised to scrub it from my memory. Which I did. I can't help what's happening now. I'm having an anti-amnesia flashback."

She said nothing, but I felt the heat of her glare. When I glanced over at her, she narrowed her eyes.

"Yeah. Not sorry. I promise never to mention it to anyone else, but now that we're safely out of the woods and the snowbank, fair warning: I'm never *ever* forgetting that."

"Ugggh." She let out a cute little growl and folded her arms over her chest again.

But when I stole another glance at her, the corners of her lips twitched. I grinned wide. "Ha! You're so busted. You've committed every damn moment of that experience to memory. Even the whole pee-in-the-cup thing."

"Maybe."

Oh, she definitely had. So had I.

Couldn't have planned it better. On a trip with a tight time schedule, when the whole point was to make new memories to top the old, to eradicate the hold my subconscious had in my sleep, the universe had thrown us a curveball we hadn't expected.

And the moments we'll have to remember from it? Perfect.

6. A MICHAELSON NEW YORK MINUTE

Nothing ever prepared me for the rush when the buildings came into view. Grand relics of an era past, housing some of the city's oldest families, watched over her park.

Fifth Avenue.

Awestruck.

Every single time.

And now that I'd brought Hannah here? Even better. There was an air of mystery about this place. Fortunes were made and lost, reputations rose and fell. Yet through it all, the city still stood proudly. And in this stretch of Manhattan's Upper East Side, she put on her best show.

Limestone-clad buildings towered over us. Central Park spanned to our right as we approached. Hannah's gasp as she rolled down the window and leaned out to look up said it all.

Energy vibrated here. Horns honked. People hustled.

And it seemed the perfect place to reset myself from whatever it was that kept plaguing me.

"Your parents live here?"

"*Lived*. Before I was born. By the time I became a blip on their radar, they'd outgrown a place more suited to parties for wealthy dignitaries than four screaming kids."

"So the country estate is their permanent home and they use this for...?"

"Social events. Occasional parties. Dad sometimes meets clients in the city and he and Mom will go out with other couples to The Met."

"The Met." Her brow infinitesimally furrowed. "The museum or the opera?"

"Either. Depends on their mood and the event schedule."

"Wow." Her voice held a breathless note as she slowly turned in her seat, taking it all in.

I grinned, loving that her first impression paralleled my every-time love of the place. "Relax. We've made it. Middle of the night still gives us plenty of time to sleep and fit in my agenda."

"Agenda?" She poked my rib. "I think we need to revise this whole 'no revealing the itinerary' rule."

"What's in it for me?"

"You need something in it?"

I leaned over as I pulled up to the curb, whispering in her ear, "I need something in you."

"Ahhh...persuasion by seduction." Her lips curved into a sexy smile. "I'm certain I could 'coerce' you into talking."

"Oh, like you'll play interrogator to my spy? I'm liking this role-play game." I nipped her earlobe, tugging it into my mouth.

The building's doorman, the same happy face who'd greeted me nearly every night I'd crashed here when in the city, approached the car. I jumped out of the driver's door, then greeted him. "Hello, Anthony."

His eyes widened in surprise. "Mr. Michaelson. Very good to see you, sir. May I take your bags?"

"Nah." I gave him a friendly handshake, then checked for traffic, rounded the back of the car, and opened Hannah's door. She took my offered hand as I guided her up out of the Mustang and around to the sidewalk. "Hannah, this is Anthony. He's been here for decades. Probably as old as this building."

"Only thirty-two years on my watch, sir. The building's been standing since 1927."

Leave it to Anthony to couple proper speech with factoids. "Anthony, this is my wife, Hannah."

He gave her a polite nod, then held out a black-gloved hand toward me. I handed him the keys.

Hannah wandered down the sidewalk, staring up at all the stately buildings, then spun in a slow circle to take in a full three-sixty, including the edge of the park at night. A horse-drawn carriage clopped by.

She threw her arms out, then took a step toward me. "The buildings are so *beautifully* maintained. There's excited buzz all around, yet time seems to stand still here. Is that what they mean by a New York minute? Like all these things fit into a second...yet it's an eternity?"

I shook my head trying not to laugh at her Mach-speed chatter. "I think a New York minute is an instant. A flash, and then it's over."

She scrunched her face. "That sucks. Who wants to lose a moment like that? Remember when we redefined redundancy?"

"Sure do." Before Christmas, in the idyllic moments when we'd been reunited—after thinking we'd lost each other for the second time in our lives—we'd decided repeating amazing moments was very necessary.

"Well, we're redefining a New York minute. It can be a *Michaelson* New York minute."

"Sounds perfect." I grinned and pulled her into my arms, kissing her softly. I would never tire of hearing her talk about being a Michaelson, or watching her spin the world into a different, amazing perspective.

After grabbing our few bags and walking through the front door Anthony held open, we made our way to the elevators (I'd politely insisted to Anthony that we'd manage on our own), then punched the up call button.

Once inside, as the doors closed, I pressed the *P* on the top of the panel.

"Of course," Hannah remarked with a smile, nodding toward the penthouse button I'd pushed.

I shrugged. "Mom came from money. This was actually an inherited property from her mother: my feisty high society grandmother, God rest her soul."

The doors opened into the polished wood space of a round entry area, which led to the double doors of the apartment. When I opened them, Hannah walked forward beside me as if she was in a trance: eyes wide, mouth slowly dropping open.

"Holy...wow." She kept walking, past my mother's favorite Chippendale tea table, over the eighteenth-century Aubusson rug, into the main living room under the plastered groin-vaulted ceiling. She stood before the window for a moment, hands hovering over the floor-to-ceiling glass in an arched alcove. When she spun around, she blinked, then made fists with her hands and exploded them open in front of her. "Just...it's so..."

"Opulent, lavish...over the top?"

The corners of her lips twitched at my amused tone, and she glanced at me. "Yes. All of that. I'm speechless." She ran

48

a finger along the top mahogany trim of an antique settee. "People actually live in places like this who aren't royalty?"

"Yeah. The upper echelon of wealth who want to be surrounded by it." I shrugged. "Mom keeps it because it's family history. Not a bad place to stay for a weekend getaway, huh?"

When all she did was shake her head and walk slowly around everything while keeping a two-foot buffer, I took her hand and wound her arm into mine. "You can touch everything. It won't bite or break. I'll give you the tour."

And so we proceeded to walk through the roughly fourteen thousand square feet of living space divided between two floors with a winding grand staircase in between. Down the hall, we approached the suite of bedrooms. I went straight for the largest guest bedroom, the only place I'd ever slept when staying over.

The mahogany sleigh bed had dark blue and green silk pillows. Matching drapes framed arched windows that stretched up to the twelve-foot coffered ceiling. A sitting area surrounded an antique Italian stone fireplace.

But Hannah never made it that far. As I slid the dimmer light switch up, an area off to the side caught her attention. A grand archway led to two areas: to her right, a marble bathroom meant to lure an unsuspecting guest to relax into oblivion, to her—

"Oh my God," she breathed, veering left. "Is...this...a *closet*?"

"It is." Two benches in plush dark green velvet sat in the center of the room. A massive tri-fold mirror arced across one corner, the other had another open archway that led to the backside of the bathroom. A crystal chandelier hung from the ceiling. An Oriental rug spanned across the floor. Dark wood drawers and doors lined the walls, with occasional lower dressers in between, which held various antiquities.

She stopped midway to the mirrored corner, then lifted her arms and spun in a slow circle. "This is *not* a closet. It's the size of my house."

"Almost. It's about a thousand square feet, give or take."

Her fingers traced the upper curve of a pewter drawer pull, then she glanced at me. "There's no way we could have sex in here."

I barked out a laugh. "Maestro, you never cease to amaze me. I'm so glad we've ruined the innocence of closets for you." I took a slow step toward her, then another, closing the distance between us. "But I'm missing the reason why we can't have sex in the most luxurious closet you're ever likely to stand in."

"It's too big."

After another long stride, I pulled her into my arms. Bending down, I growled into her ear, "I love the way you stroke my ego."

She shuddered as I ran my mouth down the slender column of her neck. "I'd love a tighter space," she murmured. "You know, we do need to keep up our claustrophobic therapy."

"Tight spaces..." I walked her backward. "You're getting warmer."

She nodded. "Me wrapped around you, clutching your shoulders..."

"Will you dig your nails in and scratch me?" I cradled her in my left arm as I swung open the large door on the right.

Her eyes widened. "Do you like that?"

"Every damn time you do."

She gasped. "I've scratched you?"

"You do all kinds of things when crazed with need: scratching, biting...screaming." I bent down, crushing her lips into a kiss until she melted against me. When I knew she'd fallen out of her head and into the moment, I dropped my hand to her hips, gripped her gently, and hoisted her into said tight space, shoving aside the clothes in the half-filled space.

Wide eyes, dilated with passion, blinked up at me. "This is..."

"A wardrobe." I closed the door with a click and darkness surrounded us.

Before she uttered a word of protest, I preemptively silenced her with another hard kiss. She moaned softly, her lips parting. Then her tongue slid forward and tangled with mine. By the time we came up for air, she was panting.

In the confines of the tight space, our breaths were the only sounds. Until her hands drifted down my abs and found by fly. The stutter of my buttons ripping open followed.

"Why, Maestro. So aggressive."

"I know what I want."

"And what's that?"

"You. In me."

"Gonna need dirtier, more specific directions."

"I'm still not wearing underwear. I'm wet and aching for you. I want you to thrust your cock inside me, until you fill me so completely, stretching me so wide and deep, I can barely pull air into my lungs."

"*Fuck.*"

Her throaty laugh echoed around us. "That *is* the idea."

I gripped her dress by the hem, stripped it up over her head, and dropped it to the floor. I skimmed my hands up her sides, then lifted her arms until my fingers slid between hers. I guided them to the solid dowel rod running across the space. "Hold on to this. Don't let go."

A cute little snort followed as I slid my hands up her thighs, lifted her legs up, and pressed her against the back wooden panel.

I smirked. "What's so funny?"

Her breath hitched as I pressed against her, my rigid cock aligning perfectly up her center. I ran my lips down her neck as I flexed my hips forward and lifted her legs higher.

She let out the softest whimper. "How will I scratch you with my nails if I'm not touching you?" Her hard swallow came seconds before the heels of her shoes dug into the top of my ass. When she eased back, a dull knock sounded behind me, but the force wasn't enough to reopen the doors.

I pressed a kiss to the base of her throat, feeling her pulse beneath my lips. "Good question. I'm willing to find out what happens when you don't get to touch..."

Then I angled her thighs higher, trapping them between our chests, before slowly thrusting inside. Without pause, I pushed in deeper. Her short gasp shot out as soon as I hit bottom. And I wasn't even all the way in yet. "You okay?"

She nodded. Or so I thought.

I paused, easing back. "Talk to me, Hannah. I don't want to hurt you."

"It's good. Intense. But good."

"Doesn't hurt?" I slid my hand away from her hip, skimming it between us until my thumb rubbed over her clit.

A low cry dragged into a whimper as she arched away from the back wall. It angled her hips, taking me deeper. I pressed small circles against her, letting her moans guide me. My cock twitched when her muscles clenched around me.

"Hurts a little" —she panted— "but in the best way." Her breath caught as another single spasm surrounded me.

"So this is good?" I flexed forward, sinking deeper in one quick slide, and pinched her clit right at the end.

Her cry was louder. "Yes. *So good.*"

Balls deep, her incredible wet heat surrounding me, it was all I could do not to lose it right there. I bent down, barely able to move in the tight space, shoulders scraping on the wood behind me. But as I sped up the rhythmic circles with my thumb, I found her nipple with my lips, sucked it in, then bit down gently with my teeth.

Her entire body shuddered, then she screamed seconds before dropping her face into the crook of my shoulder. I shot my hand back to her hip and gripped her, pulling her down onto me as I thrust up.

Teeth bit into my shoulder, not painfully, but almost. Every one of my hard thrusts tore a moan from her throat. And her orgasm kept coming, hot, tight—fucking incredible.

Still holding on to the wooden rod like an obedient girl, her sounds had reduced to soft whimpers against my skin as she rode out her every last spasm.

The next heartbeat, I sucked in a sharp breath and tensed as mine hit me, electric shock running through my balls. A low, primal growl echoed around us as I thrust one last time and came deep inside of her.

My head spun, stars fuzzing at the edges of my awareness. No idea how long we stood there. Her arms fell and wrapped around my neck. I leaned back as her legs drifted down my sides, settling around my hips.

We clung to each other. Hearts raced to catch up to our ragged breaths.

Nothing outside mattered in those seconds we'd stolen

for ourselves. Not a schedule. Not black ice. Not even elusive dreams.

I tightened my hold around her as she sighed. On a slow exhale, I pressed my lips to the top of her ear, whispering, "How was that for a Michaelson New York Minute?"

Her body shook in my arms. "Really? Confident enough to say 'minute' after quick closet sex?" Amusement tinged her voice. "And you have to ask? Were you here for what just happened?" Soft lips covered mine. She sucked and nipped in teasing kisses. "Amazing." She kissed me again. "Magnificent." Her voice lowered. "Spectacular."

When she ground her hips against me, my cock stirred back to life, and I groaned. Then I slid my lips along her jawline toward her ear, murmuring "See? It's what we do in those minutes that matter."

7. DREAMS AND
FANTASIES

After the spectacular wardrobe sex, we'd stumbled our way into the tub. Our electronics had been long forgotten along with our bags, so I had no idea what middle-of-the-night time it was.

Didn't care.

All that mattered was the woman nestled against my chest under a mountain of suds.

She slapped the surface of the water, then giggled.

All my happy-as-fuck ass could manage was a contented sigh.

My dreams wanted to fuck with me? Fine. *Bring it.*

I had the amazing therapy of Hannah in my arsenal. And this weekend was only the beginning. I mentally prepared to do battle to set myself free once and for all.

She stretched a leg up, causing white foam to slide down her olive skin from her ankle to her knee. "So if the closet is about a thousand square feet, how big is this tub?"

"It's an antique clawfoot. A larger one, though." I scanned the dimensions of the rim. "Maybe five-and-a-half feet long by almost three wide. So it's roughly sixteen square feet. About forty cubic feet."

She shifted her hips, wiggling her ass against my groin. I sucked in a fast breath as my body reacted—even after the wardrobe sex only fifteen minutes ago and the car sex a couple of hours ago.

I growled, tugging her earlobe with my teeth. "You are going to be the death of me, woman."

A satisfied humming-purr rumbled from her throat as she relaxed and wound her sudsy arms around mine, then threaded our fingers together. "What a way to go."

"Death by sex." Yep. I placed that request into the universe's suggestion box.

"And happiness." Her head slid to the side, then settled into the crook below my right shoulder.

"Where the hell are our beers? We need to toast to that."

Stillness followed. Our chests rose and fell in the same rhythm. Content, neither of us twitched a muscle to alter the zenful moment we'd found.

Until she moved her head, glancing around at the tub. "I was right. It is kind of tight."

I groaned, thoughts flashing to every way I could take her, even in this tight space. My favorite position settled to the forefront of my mind. From behind: me gripping her hips, her clutching the edge, water sloshing everywhere.

But instead of acting them out, I simply wrapped my arms tighter around her and kissed the sensitive spot on her neck that I loved so much until she shivered from the touch. "Tight is perfect. But we need rest. Sleep. We'll keep the bathtub on our list for another time."

Right now, I figured great memories from the car, the wardrobe, and the blissful time we'd spent unwinding in the hot water of the tub would translate into much-needed peaceful dreams.

I COULDN'T CATCH a full breath. Darkness closed in, comforting, yet choking. Pleasurable sensations blended with a bad gut feeling, making me uncertain about my surroundings. I reached my hands forward, trying to touch something, seeking a surface, or a light source, but nothing materialized.

In the pitch-black place, I stood alone. Fear swirled all around me, making me crazed.

"It's okay, Cade. I'm here."

Hannah's soothing voice pierced the chilling darkness. Warmth encased me. Her tropical scent drifted in as I inhaled a deep breath.

As soon as I exhaled, her presence faded. Images of the incredible sex we'd had brought the nothingness around me to life. Beds, floors, walls, closets...they all blended together until the only constant became me flexing, straining under the pressure, thrusting deep, and her arching her hips, writhing against me, riding me harder.

Our moans and gasps escalated. Hands gripped. Lips kissed. Teeth nipped.

Right as the ache intensified into near-blinding pain, when my orgasm was a split second away from the point of no return, she threw her head back and laughed. A hard shove at my chest had me stumbling backward.

A sardonic smile twisted onto the face that stared back at me. *Madison.* My ex. She shoved the ring back at me. "I don't want to spend forever with only you. Our sex isn't enough for me."

The darkness claimed me, and I fell. Down. Down. Wind whipped at me, cutting me deep. Suddenly, lots of supple curves caught me. Brunettes and blondes. A busty redhead wrapped her naked body around mine.

"I've got you, Cade. Let go," she whispered.

I did. The instant I stopped fighting, the panic began to subside.

I blinked. Even though I was still surrounded by darkness, dim light filtered in from somewhere.

I took a deep breath and exhaled as I realized Hannah's beautiful face stared back at me.

The concerned lines of her expression relaxed and she smiled. "Welcome back."

"What time is it?" I began to sit up.

She put her hand on my shoulder with her body weight behind it, and I fell back onto the bed. "Just before sunrise."

That explained the grayish glow coming in from the windows.

"You had another bad dream."

I pulled Hannah closer to me, and she turned as I tucked her into my hold. "How do you know?" On a sigh, I pressed a kiss to her shoulder blade.

She wriggled backward until her ass was firmly planted into my groin, her back flush to my chest. With every combined breath we took, the anxiety of the nightmare faded further away. She threaded her fingers with mine. "You were grunting and thrashing."

"Sounds attractive."

Her soft laughter shook her shoulders. "Oh, it was."

"I wish I could get some decent sleep, peaceful dreams."

"You will." Gentle pressure touched my forearm as a soft kiss sounded out. She rested her head against my bicep. "We just need to get through this weekend."

My brow furrowed. She made it sound like a bad thing. But although I hadn't shared details of my dreams, was sifting through the vagueness myself, she must've sensed the cause. Still, I needed to talk it out. "Because my bad dreams are tied to it?"

"Of course, they are." Her voice softened. "Cade this is a big weekend for you." She turned in my arms, touched a hand to the side of my face, then kissed me softly. "You've had a clock ticking down in your subconscious as we've headed toward Valentine's Day. The holiday had been a painful reminder of a devastating event in your life. Your dreams are you trying to move past it."

This time I kissed her on a heavy sigh. "Seems stupid to even be having them. I'm with you. I have everything I could ever want and it feels incredible. Bothers the hell out of me that my dreams can't get on board with my reality."

"Don't fight it. Let it happen. Let the wonderfulness of us overtake the rest."

The sun rose higher, bringing golden light into the room. Her steady gaze pierced straight to my heart. I saw unwavering faith and resilience there.

I grumbled, "I sound pathetic. I'm stronger than some ridiculous nightmares."

"No, babe. Our minds are powerful. You and I should know that better than most. We had to go through a lot to get our heads on straight to be together. And..."

Her pause dragged out.

I dropped my forehead to hers. "Don't hold back. I need this. You're the best kind of therapy."

"Selfish Bitch has no hold over you. This isn't about her."

The apt nickname reminder for my manipulative ex made me smile. "It isn't?"

Hannah shook her head. "No. This is about you. About

you trusting that what you have is real and won't be ripped away from you. That's what happened on Valentine's Day to you." She sat upright, folding her legs beneath her as she stared hard at me. "I'm telling you here and now—just in case there is any fragment of doubt in your mind—I'm with you for the long haul. Nothing you say could make me leave. I love you with every breath of air. Every beat of my heart is yours. Now and forever."

My heart slammed into my ribs as the force of her words hit me hard. Although I hadn't consciously doubted a thing about Hannah and me, maybe my past had tainted my ability to trust in us completely. *Utter fucking bullshit.*

I shoved up and tugged her into a fierce hug. "I love you...*more.*"

We clung to each other, high in a penthouse where family had come first for generations, sunlight now flooding into the room around us.

Our breaths were the only sound...

Then her stomach roared.

One beat...two...and we both burst out laughing.

I grabbed her hand and helped her from the bed. "C'mon. I arranged for housekeeping to shop for breakfast foods earlier this week. Let's get you fed."

After she shrugged on one of my black T-shirts, and I pulled on an old pair of Penn State sweat pants, we made our way to the kitchen.

"These tiles are freezing. *Brrr!*" She raced ahead of me. When she made it to the kitchen, she backed up against the counter, palmed the edge with both hands, and hoisted herself up after a quick jump.

I flicked on the light switch, then stared at her for a long moment. Couldn't help it. Her dark hair was tousled, all wild and framing her delicate face. Her cheeks were pinked, her eyes a vivid green, the flecks of gold in them sparking under the bright pendant lighting. The black T-shirt had fallen off one of her shoulders, the bottom of the V-neck snagged on one of her breasts.

Then I eyed the white marble countertop and arched a brow. "So instead of your feet being cold, you opted for your ass?"

She gave me a half shrug. "I'm sure you'll warm me later. Now? Feed me."

"Yes, ma'am."

I pulled open the refrigerator door. Stark shelves stared back at me. A lonely orange juice carton on the left of the top shelf balanced out an egg carton two shelves down to the right. The meat drawer held one package of bacon.

About to pull the eggs out, I growled, "*Fuck.*"

"What's wrong?"

I punched the date on the package with my fingertips, shoving the carton back a few inches. "Eggs expired two days ago. There's no bread. No fruit. They clearly misunderstood my detailed list."

"Or there was a mad run of breakfast foods at the market. Is that bacon?" She leaned to the side, trying to peer around me.

"I'm not feeding you just meat." I tried to gutter that in my mind and failed. I scowled, pissed as hell that all she'd eaten since lunch yesterday was a can of almonds. I yanked open the bottom freezer drawer. "Aha!" I grabbed two boxes and held them up. "Pizzas for breakfast."

She grinned. "All the major food groups." She pointed to the one on the left, a large supreme with meat and veggies.

I handed the other box to her, tossing the supreme onto the counter. "Plus pepperoni, your fav."

Flipping the box over, she read the directions, "Preheat

the oven at four hundred degrees. Keep pizza frozen while preheating." She mumbled the rest, about removing the packaging, before she put the box on the counter. "Then cook for eighteen to twenty minutes."

I turned the oven on, then grabbed two glasses from the cabinet beside the fridge and poured us each large orange juices. I downed half of mine while she sipped hers, then set my glass down. "Gotta be something else here to snack on while we wait." I began opening other cabinet doors. "Box of crackers, questionable age. Soup. Applesauce. Peanut butter. Tuna."

A dry laugh huffed out behind me. "Sounds like a survivalist's pantry."

Yeah. Didn't bother looking at the dates—wasn't interested.

Ignoring the "keep pizza frozen" instruction, she ripped open the boxes. Crinkling followed while she removed plastic wrap. Before she finished with the first one, I pulled out two large plates for her to put the pizzas on and slid them onto the counter. Then I opened another cabinet. Spices.

And one very interesting condiment.

Nooo...

Oh, *fuck* yes. Finally the universe had thrown me a bone. I smirked, thoughts guttering. "Does honey ever go bad?" Not that it mattered. I was willing to risk it.

"No. Honey's one of those rare foods that never goes bad as long as it's pure."

Not a damn thing pure about to happen here...

I pulled the unopened jar off the shelf and turned around. She straightened more upright on the counter, her gaze pegged on to mine. Then her attention drifted down to what I held in my hand. That sexy luscious lower lip of hers got tugged in by her teeth.

I smirked. "Care to be the appetizer?"

She sucked in a sharp breath, releasing the hostage lip. Then she gave me a slow nod.

"Shirt off." I took a step closer, then stopped, watching her.

A naughty smirk kicked the corner of her lips up. In slow motion, she stretched her arms down, grabbed the hem, then pulled it up. The material dragged up her body revealing the flare of her hips, the dip at her waist, then the lower curves of her breast, which led to hardened pink nipples. Once she reached her chin, she ripped the fabric free from her shoulders and head before tossing it behind her to catch on the corner of a barstool.

The preheat timer chimed out. I absently opened the oven door, shoved both pizzas in, and set the timer for eighteen minutes. Then I shot my attention back toward the incredibly sexy naked woman perched on the edge of the counter.

I took another step toward her while unscrewing the cap off the honey. "Would you grab me a spoon? Drawer behind your left knee."

She arched a brow but slid her leg aside a few inches, spreading her legs a little wider, before she pulled the drawer open and bent over.

Could I have gotten it? Yeah. But why rob myself of watching her?

The view? Fucking magnificent. Head down, ends of her hair brushing the tops of swaying breasts...

Widened dark eyes glanced up at me as she offered me a teaspoon. "Will this do?"

"Perfect." I took it. "Now lean back. Plant your palms on the counter behind you."

She did as requested. Causing those gorgeous breasts to jut out.

I dipped the spoon, submerging it completely. Body painting? One coat. The thicker the better. When I pulled it out, I dragged the back of the spoon along the rim, scrapping off the excess.

Her breath shallowed, chest rising and falling with every short inhalation. Her gaze locked on to the glob of honey clinging to the spoon. I raised it above her, tilting it almost upright once it hovered over my target.

A strand of thick amber hit the upper slope of her breast, then trailed down. With great focus, I followed the artistic falling line, dripping more honey onto the leading edge, as it approached her hardened nipple. My short breaths matched hers. I swallowed hard, mesmerized by the rapid rise and fall of those incredible curves.

Once the sticky trail hit her hardened peak, I pulled the spoon away.

Then I watched.

We both did.

A long, slow drip stretched down off the tip.

Fucking lost, I growled low and dove my face down. But before I made contact, I shot a quick glance up. Her eyelids had fallen half closed, eyes darkened, like the heady anticipation had drugged her.

She was fucking beautiful: blushed pink skin, dark hair wild, body spread wide.

Trusting me to take care of her.

I stuck out my tongue and caught the falling drip of honey, then rose higher until I licked over her nipple. Sweet, soft, rigid. *More.* Raw need drove me to tug it into my mouth, sucking hard, catching it between my teeth.

Her quick gasp dragged out into a low moan. When I bit down gently, her sound lowered into a raspy groan. As I lapped up her sweetness, ache speared into my cock, her crazed pleasure ramping up mine.

Her legs tightened around my hips. Fingers stabbed into my hair, began tugging at the roots, stinging my scalp, as she pulled me against her. She squirmed on the counter as I took my time, teasing and taunting this one nipple, alternating between flicking the trapped tip with my tongue and sucking hard.

Her eager gasping moans increased, like she was getting close.

And I hadn't even gotten started.

Fuck props and condiments.

I tossed the spoon onto the counter, its loud clank quickly lost in Hannah's whimpering sounds. Then I pinched her other nipple before cradling her breast in the palm of my hand.

With every suck and nip, her fevered sounds grew louder. And still it wasn't enough.

I dropped both hands down to her knees. Then I slid them up her trembling thighs, gently spreading them wider. Satisfied I had her hovering right on the edge of orgasm, I abandoned her breast and dipped lower.

I checked my self-control, slowing the fuck down with a shaky deep breath. Then I gripped her legs, opened my mouth over her center, and exhaled, fogging hot breath over her glistening pink skin.

Her hips arched upward, toward my mouth.

"Uh-uh-uh..." I gripped her thighs harder, holding her

immobile. "I'm cooking for you this morning. Only one chef in charge at a time…"

The second she relaxed, I swiped a broad tongue through her wetness. When I reached the hardened nub of her clit, I circled once, then pressed my teeth down around it and sucked in, hard and slow.

Her escalating moan echoed off the hard surfaces of the kitchen.

Fuck. Her needy cry killed me, made me harder. And yet I didn't want to take. No matter how intensely I ached to rip down my sweat pants and thrust deep into her, this moment was about her. Giving her what she needed…*then* feeding her.

I grinned and flicked my tongue out, then sucked, long and slow. After a few seconds, I began a massaging rhythm, alternating soft and hard, slow and fast—taking my time.

Her fingers stabbed back into my hair, pulling at the roots. Her head thrashed back and forth, the ends of her hair lashing my shoulders. Her thighs trembled nonstop, her hips fought my restraining hold.

And those incredible erotic noises dragged out between her every gasping breath.

I was so fucking turned on, if I'd had less control, I would have come before her.

All of a sudden, her entire body tensed. The sexy-as-fuck sounds paused. Then a piercing scream ripped from her throat.

Before her earsplitting wail finished, the oven timer joined in with its high-pitched tone.

My muffled chuckle vibrated against her before I gave a final firm, long lick. Then I pulled back and smacked her ass cheek.

On a long exhale, her upper body collapsed onto the counter, arms flung wide, dark hair fanned around her head. She looked glorious, flushed and breathless.

I smirked. "Hannah's done."

8. WICKEDLY NAUGHTY

F riday's daytime scheduled events of Fifth Avenue shopping and the American Museum of Natural History got scrapped in favor of spending the day in bed: mostly lazing in each other's arms, sometimes dozing off for *dreamless* naps. *Thank fuck.* We did manage to work in a relaxing late lunch and dessert at Serendipity 3, something I'd insisted on after she gushed about the movie *Serendipity*.

But now? We were going to the one musical I'd promised her under a gazebo so long ago.

We'd rushed into the lobby just before the show's start time. After checking our coats at the cloakroom, we hurried up the escalators, taking the steps two at a time. When we reached the top, the carpeted outer hall had been deserted except for a few employees.

One of the ushers waved us forward with a rolling hand gesture. "Are you in the orchestra section?"

"Yes." I remembered something mentioned about the orchestra when I bought the tickets.

"Hurry and I can still seat you. Had you been five minutes later, you'd have had to wait. Doors to this section remain shut until twenty minutes after curtain rise." The gentlemen looked at our tickets, escorted us to the correct entrance doors, then led us down the aisle to our row.

Our seats were located in the middle of a tight row that had promised fantastic legroom. The booking agent must've meant in comparison to other theatres, because all seven people in our path had to stand to let us by.

Finally, we found our padded seats. Odd, I distinctly remembered Hannah promising a ride during the musical. I glanced up in irritation at the box seats that had been sold out for months.

Hannah gripped my arm. Her expression was suddenly panic stricken. "I have to pee."

I tried not to smirk as I slid my hand into hers. "I don't mind being late."

She gave out a frustrated little growl, then stood in a huff.

Every damn one of the seven who'd let us pass the first time, gave us either surprised or indignant looks. The older woman's scowl with narrowed eyes made me think she wanted to charge us toll for safe passage.

When we passed back through the doors, we got our warning. "The performance starts in two minutes. There'll be no going back in until after 8:20 p.m."

Hannah shook her head, not seeming to care. "Where are the bathrooms?"

He pointed beyond the escalators.

She spun around, jogged down the hall in her four-inch heels, then began racing up the steps.

"Slow down. No twisted ankles." I followed after her up the steep carpeted stairs, planning to catch her if she tumbled back down.

About five minutes later when she reemerged from the bathroom, I inhaled a slow breath.

She looked fucking amazing. Hair tousled. Cheeks pinked. And I hadn't even laid a hand on her...yet. My thoughts drifted to how she'd look after I'd gotten done with her.

Those glossed lips twisted into a playful smirk. "What?"

"You are gorgeous."

Her sexy smile widened. Then her gaze dropped down my body. "You look quite dashing yourself, Mr. Michaelson." She stepped closer, running her hands up my chest. "It really turns me on when you dress up."

"Oh?" I leaned down, whispering into her ear. "We have almost twenty minutes. Maybe you can show me just how turned on you are."

She pulled back, frowning. "I can't believe we're going to miss the beginning. It's so good."

I dropped her a deadpan look. "You know I'm not here for the musical, right?"

Then she bit that luscious fucking lip of hers. Yeah, she knew. I grabbed her hand and carefully guided her down the treacherous stairs from the bathroom level.

When we made it back onto the second floor, she collided into my side, whisper fierce. "What are you doing?"

I arched a brow. "What do you think I'm doing?"

She blinked, then glanced at the closed doors. "But we can't go back into the theatre."

Snorting, I gave her a stern look. Maybe her innocence had trumped her naughty tonight. I intended to have her catch up. "No way is this happening in the middle of that theatre."

Her eyes widened.

I raised my brows in amusement. Yeah. *Now* she was with the program.

Instead of the escalator, we took the wider stairs back down to the main lobby. Less dangerous, more fun.

When we reached the bottom, Hannah stole a glance at me, then stared up at the ceiling in thought. "That's a lot of Michaelson New York minutes in our twenty. Like a thousand or more, right?"

I chuckled, then kissed her. "Something like that."

At the cloakroom, the girl who'd taken our coats earlier glanced up. "Back so soon?"

"My wife...needs something from her coat."

Hannah shot me a death glare.

When the girl turned to retrieve it, I leaned forward, "Miss?" I extended a folded hundred dollar bill in my hand. "She'll need to look for it herself. And I would *really* like to help her."

The girl's gaze locked on to the clear bribe. "I'm not supposed to let anyone back there."

"You aren't going to. We were never here."

She finally smiled and slipped the money from my fingers. "I do have a distracting boyfriend who I need to have a long text conversation with."

I grinned. "Good. Because we might be 'never here' for a while."

The cloakroom wasn't fancy, because no one was ever supposed to see it behind the scenes. Rows of wooden hangers with numbered tickets held coats of every type.

Hannah backed toward one of the corners, behind a line of wool, nylon, and fur sleeves. "We are *not* having sex in a coat closet at the Gershwin Theatre."

"We're not?" I stalked her from the other side of the coat lineup while I glanced along the ceiling edge. A security camera was mounted into a corner, but the long rack of coats blocked her from view from the neck down.

As I rounded the end of the garment rack, I caught sight of her again. She'd found an upholstered chair that she stood in front of. One of her feet rested barefoot on the seat cushion.

She gave a slow headshake. "No." Mischief sparked in her eyes.

Confused, I furrowed a brow. "What are we doing then?"

She reached back, causing the fabric of her low-cut black dress to pull taut across her breasts. The slow, faint sound of zipper ticking open followed. "I'm going to undress."

"I like where this is going..."

"And you're going to watch." Her tone had lowered, soft, sensual.

Cock hardening, I smirked. "I like this game."

One of her hands slid up her calf, then trailed over her thigh, taking the fabric of her dress with it. In teasing slow inches, she bared the entire side of her leg until she reached her hip. A thin scrap of lace clung to her there.

She paused.

My gaze shot up to hers.

The look she shot back was hungry, filled with need.

Oh, fuck yeah. We were *so* having sex. She only wanted to offer me a tantalizing preview.

I dropped my hands into my pockets. Only way I could keep them under control.

Her gaze held mine for another beat before a seductive smirk curved one side of her lips. Then she turned slightly, offering me a view of her backside. She lifted the dress higher, grabbing it with her other hand, baring her sinfully sexy ass. A black lace thong lay across her smooth skin, an erotic roadmap begging to be traced.

In slow motion, her head dropped to the side, exposing her neck. "Help me with my dress?"

Could we have left it on? Sure. Would she have been more comfortable with the risk of someone walking in? Definitely. But she offered me something more. Her vulnerability. Her trust. A sensual encounter to imprint into both of our memory banks for the rest of our lives.

One chance. This moment.

All we ever had.

Carpe fucking *diem.*

I yanked my hands out of my pocket and closed the distance between us, more than happy to help. The instant my body pressed flush with hers, she leaned back against my chest. Her face tilted up as her eyes fluttered shut and her lips parted.

Sliding my hands over her shoulders, down her arms, I dropped my mouth to hers. But I didn't kiss her. Breathing in her amazing scent, I brushed my lips across hers. Teasing. Taunting.

The dress slid lower, lower still, until it caught on her hip with her leg still raised.

Bending down, I hovered my lips over the graceful line of her neck. At first, only my hot breath touched her, then my lips in occasional tender kisses. At the curve where her neck met her delicate collarbone, I drew the soft skin into my mouth.

Her low gasp filled my ears.

Then I slid a hand under her thigh, lifting her leg slightly before guiding it off the chair. When she lowered her foot and stepped back into her shoe, the dress drifted down, finally pooling at her feet. She wound her hands along my arms, tilting her head to the side. Her eyes were still closed, long dark lashes brushing the tops of her cheeks. Her chest rose and fell with her excited breaths. The skin above the scalloped lace of her bra, up her neck, and on her face had flushed pink with her arousal.

I had the woman of my dreams standing in my arms, offering herself to me.

My woman—my wife.

The moment crystallized into what it was: a rare gift.

A New York minute was only an instant. Our time together would last forever.

Honored to be here with her, I ran my hands along her body. Soft skin. Toned muscles.

I dragged my lips up the column of her neck again. She shivered when I kissed her earlobe. Then I sucked it into my mouth, tugged it gently with my teeth. I growled low, "Telling me I can't have something with you only makes me want it more."

My fingers of one hand slid under the lace strap of her thong, gliding along her hipbone. But I left it there. With the other, I reached around, skating across the top of her bra, slipping my fingers under the flimsy fabric, until they brushed across her hardened nipple.

I pinched it.

She groaned low.

Her head was turned toward me over her shoulder, her mouth within reach. I captured her lips in a hard kiss.

Then I gave her a filthy itinerary. "We won't have sex here, Hannah. I'm not going to make slow love to you. I'm going to fuck you. Hard. And I won't ask permission." Didn't need to. She'd already given it with her body.

And it *was* making love. Every time we touched, it was heartfelt—soul-searing.

The only difference was letting our carnal sides out to play.

She made no move. Gave no protest.

When I pulled back, unzipped my pants, and caught the heavy erection that sprang free, she shivered in the cool air. Then I covered her body again with mine. With kisses down her spine, I coaxed her upper body forward until the angle forced her to throw her arms out and brace her hands on the top of the chairback. Now that she was free from her dress, I slid a hand down the back of her thigh, then lifted her leg until she rested her bare foot on the cushion once more.

With my fingers back under the lace strap of her thong, I pulled it aside. Then I thrust forward, gliding my cock through her slick folds. Oh, she was turned the fuck on, all right—she was dripping wet. A couple of quick thrusts drenched my length.

Tiny whimpers came from her throat. Her body trembled with anticipation, primed for me.

I eased back and caught the tip at her entrance, but then waited there. On a slow exhale, I pressed in only about an inch.

Fuck. I pinched my eyes shut from the heady pleasure shooting through me.

Leaning forward, I covered her upper body with mine, gripping her hips. After a shaky breath, I pressed a kiss to her shoulder blade, then whispered, "Not a sound."

Her single nod followed.

Then I drove forward, burying myself fully into her.

She gasped and pushed the chair, knocking the top into the wall.

We stayed there, breathing heavy, locked together in the epic sensual moment. Until I drew backward, torturously slow. When I'd almost pulled out, with my tip gripped tight just inside her entrance, I paused. Then I drove my hips forward again.

She groaned low at the jarring impact, but arched her back, angling for more.

I smoothed a palm down her spine, eased back, and thrust forward. Hard. Then I began a pounding rhythm, slowly drawing my hips away before every forceful thrust.

Hannah looked fucking incredible with her sensual curves, breasts swaying—beauty in motion.

On a sudden gasp, she turned her face to the side, pressing her mouth against her shoulder to quiet a long moan. Her grip tightened on the chairback, knuckles turning white.

Seconds later, heat flooded around me and I gave a single harder thrust, seating deep inside. Her muffled scream followed as her hard spasm gripped me before wave after wave clenched my cock.

I sucked in a sudden lungful of air as ache shot through me. Unable to hold back, blood roaring in my ears, I gripped her hips, holding on, as a powerful orgasm overtook me.

The room spun around us as I settled over her, wrapping my arms around her, holding on to the only thing in the world that grounded me.

Our heavy breaths slowly settled. Rapid heartbeats began to calm.

I pressed a soft kiss to her shoulder blade.

She giggled and her shoulders shook as I slipped from her body.

"What's so funny?" I grinned. Couldn't help myself.

"I really *do* need to grab something from my coat now. *Tissues* anyone?"

———

YEAH, okay. *Wicked* was actually a decent musical, the last three-quarters of it, anyway. And what we'd paid attention to. Because we'd kept stealing heated glances at each other, like high school teenagers on a first date. Didn't matter that we'd already had incredible sex. We were riding high on the euphoria of it: that we'd snuck away and had our own private show, that it had been an intensely emotional moment for us, that we'd gotten away with it without being discovered.

As promised, the coat-check girl had kept busy with her boyfriend texting while standing guard outside. She'd even had the courtesy to stick earbuds into her ears and listen to music loud enough that I'd been able to make out the song as we left the cloakroom.

When we returned for our coats after the performance, I handed her the claim ticket with a nonchalant expression and an extra twenty. She fought a smile as she disappeared into the room. When she returned it was all business, handing us our coats, then helping the next in the crowd of people behind us.

Once we'd made it out to the sidewalk, I wrapped an arm around Hannah's shoulder. Walking away from the dispersing crowd into the crisp night air was a welcome relief from the stifling bottleneck of people inside.

She nudged into my side with a hip bump. When I glanced down, she beamed a smile at me. "Well, what do you think?"

I swallowed a laugh. "About musicals? Or cloakrooms?"

She smirked. "Both."

"Not bad. And fucking amazing. Literally." I squeezed her shoulder when she giggled, and her cheeks blushed a gorgeous shade of pink. "But I'm not doing either again. Ever."

"Why?" Her brows drew together.

"Because the one musical was all I'd agreed to. Once is enough."

"And the cloakroom?"

I spun her around and gathered her into my arms. Then I slowly walked her backward, dropping my mouth to her ear. "The cloakroom was perfect. No encore could ever top it."

I STARTLED AWAKE. Hannah jolted upright on a gasp. I almost dove out of bed to do battle with an intruder. Then I remembered.

No bad dream. *Thank fuck.*

Not an intruder either.

She'd been shocked by my early-morning surprise.

"Cade," her breathless whisper was followed by her hand clutching my forearm.

I pushed myself up from the bed and wrapped my arms around her. "You slept like the dead this morning, so I was able to sneak them in."

She blinked twice at me. Then she scanned the room, starting from the bedside table. On every square inch of surface space stood a crystal vase with a dozen red roses.

Her voice held an awestruck note. "All of them? When? There has to be twenty bouquets. Did you have a crew of helpers?"

"Twenty-two dozen. And nope. No way in hell I'd let anyone in while you were sleeping. They left the entire delivery in the outer vestibule. Then I carried them in one at a time. Had to pull in a few extra pedestal tables from the guest rooms."

She lunged toward me, kissed me hard, then pulled away, looking around again. "Just...wow. I love them. Thank you."

I tucked a finger under her chin, angling her face back toward me. "Happy Valentine's Day, Maestro." After a slow inhale, I bent down and captured her lips in a soft kiss. "And you're welcome. It was the only way I could bring you a meadow of flowers."

When I pulled away, her eyes sparkled with moisture. "Like the meadow at the park. Be careful, Mr. Michaelson. You're ruining me for all other ways of receiving flowers."

I chuckled. "I seriously doubt that. You act like a kid with even a single flower."

My heart kicked as I remembered moments in the past year with her and flowers—including our first unexpected "I love you."

She launched from the bed and began touching the red velvet buds, burying her face in one flower, then another, as she inhaled their sweet scents that drifted all around us.

And I exhaled in relief, grateful for this moment.

9. ANOTHER DETOUR

The rest of Saturday turned into another lazy day—the perfect kind. Breakfast? We ordered in. Lunch? We wandered to the noisy Jewish deli a few blocks down. But dinner? Oh, you bet we had a reservation for dinner...and very special after-dinner plans that Hannah had no clue about.

Arm in arm, we passed the line of waiting horse-drawn carriages. Hannah nudged into my side. "Doesn't that look romantic?"

I didn't bother to look. "No. Riding in a cart with a blanket half the city has been under, behind an animal with a bag of horseshit strapped to its ass? I'll pass."

Her shoulders shook with laughter. "You paint the most beautiful pictures."

I kissed the top of her head. "I have something much more romantic in mind for later."

When we stepped into Anton's, the frenzied atmosphere of New York mellowed into an escape to southern Italy. Aromas of their famed savory dishes flooded my senses, making my mouth water. From speakers hidden in the rafters, Frank Sinatra serenaded the guests. Even the host behind the podium had a chilled vibe, calmly juggling tables, waitstaff, and reservations.

He scanned down the list. "We do not have a Michaelson this evening."

The mellow music screeched to a halt in my head. All the calm? Gone. Silverware clanked on dishes. Busboys hustled to clear tables. Two dozen waiting customers were crammed into the tiny lobby area, which had seating accommodating only eight.

I leaned toward the host, growling, "Check again."

He held my gaze for a beat longer, then humored me. This time he flipped to the second page, as if 7:00 p.m. might've been mistaken for hours later. When he reached the bottom, he took a deep breath, then cast an apologetic look at me. "I'm very sorry, sir. Could it have been made for another night?"

"Does Valentine's Day fall on another night?"

He never took his eyes off me, but I could tell he was thinking. Poring through his damned book would do neither of us any good. Didn't matter. He had two customers on one of their busiest nights of the year without a table. The reasons were irrelevant.

"Let me see what I can do," he offered. Then he glanced past us at the three couples waiting to check in. Translation: after I help everyone else who'd been lucky enough to be written in on the correct day, I'll see if I can't shove you into a table by the kitchen.

Uh, fuck no.

"Is your maître d' here tonight?" I didn't step aside. We weren't done yet.

"Of course, sir."

"What is his name?"

82

"George Millieu. But he's very busy tonight."

I leaned closer, lowering my voice. "Will you please tell Mr. Millieu that Kincade Michaelson is here? Son of Victoria and Garrett Michaelson. Grandson of Irene Morgan. All of whom have dined here loyally for decades with royalty and politicians."

His eyes widened a fraction at the dismissive misstep he'd almost made. "Absolutely, sir. Give me a moment."

Hannah glanced back at the growing line, then up at me, whispering, "That was quite impressive."

I gave her a half shrug. "I don't name drop unless absolutely necessary."

Seconds later, the host returned with the maître d', a thin-built man with intelligent eyes behind wire-rimmed glasses.

"Mr. and Mrs. Michaelson." He held out a hand, which I took. "We're very honored to have you join us tonight." He gave me a firm handshake, then nodded and gestured for us to move toward the potted plant nearest the dining room, away from the crowded lobby.

I put my hand behind Hannah's lower back and escorted her to the apparent clandestine discussion about to take place.

"My sincerest apologies for the misunderstanding. How long have you been waiting?"

"About ten minutes at the podium."

"Would you be willing to wait another fifteen? We have access to the rooftop for very important guests, but the table needs to be set up."

When I glanced at Hannah, her excited expression told me her unequivocal vote. I turned back toward George. "Open-air rooftop? Are there heaters?"

He tipped his head in a reverent nod. "Yes. I assure you it will be a worthy substitute."

"Thank you, George. We would love a rooftop table."

Fifteen minutes dragged into twenty-three. But with every new couple who crammed into Anton's from the cold, their reservations merely granting them growing wait times, I was grateful we had a table at all. Even if the universe at large had tried to rob us of one.

Finally, a gentleman in a classic black-and-white uniform approached us. "Mr. and Mrs. Michaelson?"

Hannah turned toward him as I gave a nod.

"I'm Joseph, your server for the evening. If you'll come this way, I'll escort you to your table. Please pardon the unusual scenery en route."

As he led the way and we followed, I realized "unusual" was a unique way of describing it. We were led out the back kitchen door, down a narrow, sterile hallway, to the building's service elevator. Once we all stepped inside, he pressed the *R* button at the top, above the other fourteen numbered floors. When the elevator doors reopened, we stepped onto the expansive rooftop terrace.

I blinked. Once. Then again.

Hannah gasped. "Oh my God."

A quick glance toward the low parapet wall surrounding the space confirmed my eyes weren't deceiving me; we were indeed on the top of a building. The brightly lit New York skyline spanned to the south and the dark swath of Central Park ran northward, down Fifth Avenue on the right.

But as our waiter led us forward, a hidden paradise unfolded in every direction. Rock formations to our immediate left created the beginning of a brook, complete with babbling sounds. The waterway flowed through lush vegetation. Stones near the water were covered with moss. Deep green ferns fluttered in the slight breeze, hinting at a rainbow of flowers beyond them. Trees whose trunks were wrapped with white lights had branches devoid of leaves that reached up toward the cloud cover. At the far end, a wading pool complete with sandy beach and Adirondack chairs rested peacefully, but the rolled white towels on the table near the chairs seemed to be taunting visitors to swim.

Hannah pulled me ahead, carefully negotiating across flat, gray stepping stones edged by spongy dark green moss. Ambient warmth from heaters disguised as botanical spires, placed every dozen feet or so, kept the entire area comfortable.

"This place is unreal," she whispered.

I exhaled a breath I'd probably been holding since we stood at the podium, worried the night had been derailed.

Then I grinned. We'd kept hitting obstacles, yet things continued to work themselves out—vastly toward the better. I'd never considered myself an optimist. Realist suited me better. But I found myself drinking the half-full glass and subscribing to the notion. Maybe the point to focus on wasn't the shit life threw at you, but the great things you did in spite of it.

I took another look at the tempting wading pool. The air was mild up on the roof with all the heaters, but we were dressed up and I had other plans for us. While the waiter stood patiently beside our table, letting us take our time through the intimate garden, I gathered Hannah into my arms from behind and nodded toward the pool. "How 'bout we make plans to come back here sometime. No dinner, maybe just dessert..."

Her soft laugh danced in my ears as she turned toward me. "What? No spontaneity? No skinny dipping?"

I gave her a slight headshake and kissed her softly. "Not

now. Tonight you'll have to settle for a tamer version of your husband. We've got more plans to come, and I want to be sure you're not freezing your ass off." Or that we weren't any later than we'd already be.

Finally, walking hand in hand, we crossed over to our waiting table. From fifteen feet away, a tree's branches reached almost overhead, tiny white lights strung along its trunk and skeletal canopy. In the center of the table, a flickering trio of tea light candles floated amid red rose petals in a shallow bowl.

After I held the chair out for Hannah, then sat myself, Joseph handed us menus that had a slender parchment paper clipped to the top. "You may choose the Valentine's Day three course special or select from the menu. Please take your time. I'll wait in the garden until you decide." He retreated about a dozen paces back.

I scanned down the holiday menu: baby arugula and wild mushroom salad with a truffle dressing or butternut squash and roasted red pepper soup; prosciutto, artichoke, and garlic stuffed ravioli in a white wine sauce; house-made chocolate gelato with raspberries. I glanced up at her. "What would you like?"

She grinned, setting down her menu. "I will always choose the chef's special on a holiday."

"Ahhh, your culinary roots are showing." I waved Joseph over, then gave him our order plus requested a bottle of the artisanal wine they'd paired with the dish.

After Joseph left, Hannah slipped her hands into mine. I lifted one to my mouth, brushing a soft kiss across her knuckles.

We chatted about small things while we waited for our food: her favorite flower from the rooftop garden, which musical she'd want to actually *see* if we ever went to another,

her plans to chart a five-star Zagat tour of Manhattan restaurants on our next visit.

Then we discussed the possibility of swimming in that rooftop pool tomorrow or another weekend. I leaned back, crossing my arms, giving the matter serious thought. "We'll need to find the right person to bribe for access."

The elevator doors opened, and Joseph appeared with a large tray balanced on his shoulder. Hannah tilted her head, her voice lowering. "Or learn to scale the exterior of the building."

I narrowed my eyes at her. "Woman, you continue to intrigue me."

A slow smile brightened her face. "I wouldn't have it any other way."

The meal was off-the-charts incredible. As we ate, we continued to talk about nonsensical topics: which day of the week she loved, how she'd hated celery as a child, but had come to love it, how I'd tried Nutella, repeatedly, with no idea what everyone saw in it. *Yeah, I'm a peanut butter guy.*

The conversation lulled. I sat back, sipping on wine, enjoying the night. Then my thoughts somehow spiraled down a rabbit hole: why we were here, what the holiday had been in years past, why my dreams had been plaguing me.

"Why so serious?" Hannah's humorously deep tone snapped me out of my thoughts. Amusement flickered in her darkened greenish eyes. She tried to hold her hard expression, but the twitching at the corners of her lips gave way to a smile. She arched her brows, waiting.

I shook my head, feeling like an idiot. "Sorry, babe. All the sleeplessness and dark dreams have rattled me."

With a slight head tilt, her eyes softened and she slid her hand over mine. "Don't be sorry. The power of our dreams can be unsettling—they latch on to our deepest fears. I've never shared this with you before, but I suffered from nightmares for a while after..."

Her long pause made my mind connect the dots.

"Dumbfuck?" Yep. I said it. The only way we'd ever address him. Besides, she'd pulled out Selfish Bitch yesterday. Tit for tat.

She merely gave me a stoic nod.

"But you don't have them now. Why the fuck am I having dreams related to my ex? Makes no sense." I turned her hand over in mine, sliding my fingers between hers.

"Who knows? I still have a recurring dream about being back at high school. It's my first day, and I can't find my class or don't remember my schedule. In the dream, I'm totally stressed out about it. Half the time I go through long and twisting hallways to find the front office, wait in a long line while school goes on without me, and finally request a new schedule printout."

"And the other half?"

"I go through hall after hall, searching for my locker. When I finally find it, I can't remember my combination. I'm late for class, but the book I need for it is in there. Eventually, I end up on this prolonged journey back through halls and buildings up to the front office to get my locker combination."

"That's fucked up."

She huffed out a laugh. "Tell me about it. I have a complex about front offices now. And classes. And lockers."

I thought about her dream. "The theme in both is that you're missing out on something. And no matter what you do, it's out of your reach."

"Bravo." She gave me a slight nod. "After years of that dream, I finally figured that out."

"Did it go away once you solved the puzzle?"

"No." She stared at the tablecloth in thought. "I have the dreams less often, but I still have some incarnation of it now and then. I think because I never had friends growing up. Maybe I still have the dream because I now have friends and don't want to lose them. Who knows?"

Done with our meal, I tossed my napkin onto the table. "It's driving me crazy, trying to figure out why I'm having mine."

"Tell me the details you remember. Let me have a stab at it."

Great word choice. I'd happily give her the sharpest blade to sink to the hilt into my nightmare.

I sighed. It sucked to be talking about this on our Valentine's Day. But Hannah was trying to help, and at the root of our trip, it's what we were here for. Then I tried to remember. "There aren't many details. Vague images, really. Feeling helpless and upset."

"Do you think you're still wrestling with some issue between you and her? Maybe guilt because she suffered while you were a couple, but you had no idea? Then after we got together, she reached out to you, wanting your help, but she was too far gone for you to save her?"

"Wow." I blinked hard. A part of me did feel badly for Madison. Maybe the feeling ran deeper than I gave it credit for. "But what am I supposed to do to fix that?" I needed peace. Hannah had my undying love—she had all of me. It bothered the fuck out of me that when I went to sleep, my brain grappled with shit that was out of my control.

"The only thing you can do is accept it. There's nothing you can do for Madison. It wasn't in your power to help her years ago, nor could you have done anything when she came to you over the summer."

When Hannah's hand squeezed mine, I realized my gaze

had gone unfocused over her shoulder. I shifted my attention back toward her.

Her brow furrowed, expression fierce. "Forgive yourself. That will set you free."

The thought hadn't occurred to me that I'd been subconsciously punishing myself for crimes I hadn't committed. But I had felt guilty about not being able to do more for Madison. Yet it wasn't my fault. None of it had been.

Just being aware of that fact helped ease the burden. And in those seconds, I forgave the college kid that had accidentally loved a girl without realizing she'd been broken, and I let the man off the hook who'd been blindsided by her again and had to turn her away.

Tension eased from my shoulders. "Thanks, Maestro. It's helping already. So now what?"

She gave me a warm smile. "Then embrace all of the good things in your life around you."

I stood with her hand still in mine, pulled her up from the table, and tugged her into my arms. "I will." I gave her a gentle squeeze. "Often."

A purring moan vibrated from her throat as she kissed my neck, my jaw, then my lips. "And love the ones you're with. All you can do."

I stared into her eyes, lost in the intensity radiating from them. "All I ever want to do."

She swayed in my arms and I moved with her, shifting my hands, sliding my left into hers and dropping my right to her lower back. "Care to dance?"

Her bright smile beamed up at me. "But there's no music."

Carefully negotiating us back into the manicured garden with every step and turn, I dropped my lips to her neck, brushed them up toward her ear, then whispered, "When have we ever needed music?"

Over the moss-covered stepping stones, around lighted trees, under the blanket of cloud cover that smelled of the rich mineral tang of rain yet never threatened a drop—we danced.

And as Hannah rested her head in the crook of my shoulder and I held her tightly, all the world fell away. On a magical rooftop garden, only the two of us existed.

10. FEMININE…THINGS

W hen we stepped out the front door of Anton's after dinner, Hannah pulled her coat collar tighter around her neck. The night air was warmer than the last couple of evenings, temps hovering right above freezing, but were now slowly dropping. And during our rooftop-dinner escape, the heavy cloud cover hadn't turned into a single drop of rain.

Thank you, Mother Nature.

After we'd made arrangements with the restaurant manager for a potential rooftop wading-pool visit tomorrow, Hannah and I walked along the sidewalk, hand in hand, while she commented on every little thing she noticed about the city. Occasionally, she'd get quiet. Like the last few minutes.

"You okay?"

Her brows drew together. "Yeah. It…ummm…might be a girl thing."

I had *no* idea what that meant. But if she was in distress? I wanted to fix it. "What can I do?"

"Where are we going?"

"To the park. But if you're not feeling well, we can go back to the apartment."

"No." She stared down the street, squinting. "Is there a drugstore on the way?"

Drugstore? Her words repeated in my head. A split second later the light bulb flashed on. "Ohhh...a *girl* thing." My expression relaxed. She was dealing with her time of the month. Then I went into full-blown male problem-solving mode.

I took her gloved hand in mine, then headed east. "There's one just around the corner."

The brick building still housed Arnold & Sons, a place I'd frequented in the past for various things—beer mostly. I held the door open for her.

As we strode down the main aisle, something caught my eye that would be perfect for tonight. "Mind if we split up? I'll meet you at the register up front."

Relief washed across her face. "Of course, take your time. I might be a few minutes."

In other words, she wanted a little space to get her girl things. No problem. Guys wanted to steer clear of such "things" anyway. I kissed her forehead before she headed off in the opposite direction. Every few steps, she glanced up at aisle markers to locate what she wanted. Then she turned down one of the aisles.

Good. Plenty of time for a last-minute covert op. Stealth and focus had me select my purchase, beeline for the registers, pay for it, then hide it with permission from the manager, all before Hannah returned.

I stood at the front. As the seconds stretched by, I began turning the wire carousel that held Valentine's Day cards with cheesy messages: "Be mine," "You complete me," "I've been struck by Cupid's arrow."

One even had some ripped naked guy holding a box of chocolates in front of his dick. *Really?* Because nothing says "I love you" more than a picture that screams, "Hey, have this box of appetizers before you eat the main course." And the card's model was hotter than ninety-eight percent of the male population. Which severely limited the card's buying pool.

With a grin I couldn't help, I picked up the card. Yeah, I was man enough to deliver it.

Holding my formerly purchased contraband safely inside my coat and the card in my hand, I went in search of Hannah. Even though only about seven minutes had ticked by, it felt like longer. And I wanted to be sure she didn't need anything.

There she was, standing three-quarters down aisle number eight, holding one box in each hand. Her left wrist twisted before she began reading the back of the blue box. Two others were tucked under her arm.

I glanced up at the sign. *FEMININE PRODUCTS*.

Not wanting to rush her, I stayed put, scanning the items on shelves at eye level. Hemorrhoid cream. The reminder snapped a flashback into my head—from before we'd gotten together, when all I could think about was convincing her we needed to get together—when Hannah teased me about guys who made a big deal about buying tampons and hemorrhoid cream. I grinned, remembering her sprawled on my bed, me holding her notepad hostage.

She glanced up. "Hey. I'll be right there. Just a couple more minutes."

"No problem. I'm good." And clueless about the intricacies of choosing tampons—and whatever else came with it. Not that I would make a big deal about assisting her. I would buy tampons for her. I would even buy her hemor-rhoid cream, but I sure as fuck hoped she'd never need it.

I wandered down a few aisles, then turned right. The toy aisle. A few steps in, and I got stuck in front of the Matchbox cars. Yep. I collected 'em. As a kid, anyway. But really, did we ever grow up?

In a field of about two dozen hooks filled with all different vehicle models, I stared at a horrendous neon-green truck with monster wheels. I moved each package aside, inspecting the rest of the lineup. Hidden all the way in the back by the holed pegboard, shiny black paint and a slight back fin caught my attention. I moved the others onto neighboring hooks, and there it was. A black Mustang Fast-back, a miniature version of Hannah's Josephine.

By the time I emerged from the toy aisle, Hannah stood beyond the registers.

I rushed back up front. "Did you already pay?"

With a smile, she lifted her white plastic bag.

"Well, turn around. You can't see what I'm buying." No big deal if she did. Would only get a great laugh sooner rather than later.

A few minutes later, we stepped back out onto the side-walk, the air crisper by a few degrees.

She looped her arm through mine. "Do you mind if we hit a bathroom on the way?"

I mentally sorted through our choices. Back to the drugstore; but if she'd wanted to use that, she would've mentioned something inside. The park had plenty, if she was willing to suffer through rudimentary.

The clock for the scheduled evening ticked well past our timeline—but her needs came above all else. "It's about a fifteen-minute walk back to the apartment. Want to head up there?"

After chewing on her lower lip for a minute, she nodded.

Twenty minutes of worry about her later, we entered the apartment. She kissed my cheek, then spun around and rushed down the hall toward the guest bedroom. With the five bathrooms I'd shown her on the tour, she'd apparently felt most comfortable with the familiar. Even if it was palatial.

I pulled out my phone. *Fuck.* We were over an hour late, and I hadn't thought to fire off a text at the drugstore.

Hoping my guy was still there, I rapidly typed, then hit SEND.

> Still coming. Can you wait?

A minute dragged by. Then another. Finally my phone vibrated.

> I'm here, but I need to be home in an hour.

Not enough time.

> There's an extra $200 if you can stay longer.

A bubble popped up as he typed.

> I've got a wife and two kids at home.

> Make it $300 and I'm yours as long as you need.

A toilet flushed down the hall. *My* wife. The woman I wanted and needed to take care of tonight.

> Done. We'll be there inside of thirty.

I hoped.

While I waited, I found a pen in a kitchen drawer and signed the man-candy card. I thought for a moment about the chocolate box in the image, then wrote a message.

> *Forget the chocolates.*
>
> *My woman?*
>
> *Will be treated to the main course first.*
>
> *You are dessert.*
>
> *Meant to be savored . . . Loved.*
>
> *Happy Valentine's Day, Maestro.*
>
> *Your Cade*

I walked down the hall and into the bedroom. Her black wool coat had been draped on the corner of the bed's footboard. Sounds of the faucet turning on told me I had seconds left, and I hid the card behind the vase on the nightstand. We'd pull it out for a laugh later.

The rustling of plastic caught my attention. She tied off the ends of the bag again before slipping something into the side pocket of her dress, probably reinforcement supplies for later. Then she turned and walked toward me, looking radiant. A beautiful smile curved onto her face. Her hair tumbled down to her shoulders in soft waves, like she'd just brushed it.

"You okay?" I frowned. Her needs came above all else, no matter my plans. "We don't have to go if you're not feeling up to it."

She gave me a firm headshake, then lifted her coat from

the bed. "No. I'm good. Us girls are resilient when it comes to this kind of stuff."

I took the coat from her and held it open. "Well, good. 'Cause us men are a clueless wreck about it."

When she turned around, I held up an object between us. "A small token from tonight."

She glanced down. "Awww...it's a tiny Josephine!" Grinning wide, she opened the package, admired the miniature car, then tucked it into her coat pocket.

"I'm glad you like it. Seemed a fitting reminder of Josephine in a snowbank, our first car sex ever, and her visit to New York." I wrapped her in my arms and gave her a tender kiss.

Minutes later, we walked back out from the lobby of the building onto the sidewalk.

"Feel like walking?" I glanced at her leather riding boots.

"Is it far?"

"About twenty minutes."

She blew out a breath and a puff of air clouded from her mouth. But a smile lit up her face. "Yes, please. The air is crisp. Feels like snow. Maybe." She stared up into the night sky, squinting into the starless darkness, like she could forecast by intuition.

She laced her fingers with mine as we stepped into the crosswalk that led toward Central Park. Then she leaned harder against my side.

The action calmed me, and I exhaled a slow breath as I wrapped an arm around her shoulder. I'd been more worried about her than I'd realized. She'd mentioned her period before over the months. But it was always in passing, like a coded warning to keep my distance and give her greater understanding for a few days. The event had never been front and center like tonight.

So many things had tried to derail us this weekend, but we were still here, enjoying ourselves.

In fact, that had been the story of us. One thing after another, the universe kept spinning us curveballs. And we kept knocking 'em outta the park.

I gave her a gentle squeeze. The weekend was one of a million yet to come that we'd be spending together, and we'd be happy as fuck no matter what life brought us.

Dreams trumped nightmares.

11. THE BEST FOR LAST

The walking paths through Central Park on a Saturday night normally had late-night joggers. But tonight, couples were everywhere. I hung us back from the crowds, to make sure we had at least a fifteen-foot stretch to ourselves.

Hannah slowed, matching my stride. "I like being here at night. With you."

I tugged her into a shadowed space under a tree. Bending down, I ran my lips over her ear until she shivered. I kissed the soft skin at the top. "I like being anywhere with you."

"Even when we have to make drugstore detours and bathroom pit stops?"

I pulled back with a grin, then kissed her. "Especially when all the unexpected goes down."

Widening eyes gazed up at me. "You know, you're right. So many amazing things have happened to us when we never saw them coming." She pulled me out of the alcove. "Come on, Mr. Tour Guide. I believe you have an undisclosed itinerary item to reveal."

"That I do." And a time schedule. I pulled out my phone. We had five more minutes.

Around the next bend, The Loeb Boathouse restaurant came into view. The stone columns under the patio glowed yellow with their up-lighting. The mirrored surface of the lake reflected the restaurant in perfect postcard beauty.

Hannah gasped excitedly beside me, tugging us toward the lights. "Wow. It's beautiful."

I gently pulled her back, catching her in my arms. "That's not where we're going."

"No?" She stopped, gaze full of curiosity and wonder.

Hoping she'd like what I'd arranged instead, I nodded toward the man waiting at the edge of the dock. "Your water carriage awaits."

When she turned, she gasped much slower this time. "Cade…"

The only gondola allowed on the lake hovered against the dock. Pierre, the man I'd arranged our covert ride with, stood in the classic black pants and red-and-white striped shirt, straw hat fastened to his head. He gave me a broad smile. Without pause, I slipped the folded bills into his hand, thanking him monetarily for the extra hassle.

"Mr. and Mrs. Michaelson." He tipped his head toward us. "I'm honored to be your guide this evening."

Per request, tea light candles had been lined up along the outline of the bow, a brand-new faux fur blanket lay folded in front of the two intimate seats, and a bottle of champagne sat in an ice bucket, off to the side.

"You like?"

"Oh my God." She threw her arms around me in a fierce hug. "I love!"

Wanting to be sure we didn't get dunked into the icy water, I stepped in first. Then Pierre and I both assisted her down, in front of the seats. Before the wobbling stopped, I guided her onto the seat beside me.

She tugged the blanket onto her lap, leaning toward me. "How did you arrange this? There aren't any other boats out."

Before I answered, Pierre gently pushed us away from the dock with the oar. "Wasn't easy. But the boathouse manager and Pierre are both romantics, and I convinced them that with the warm winter temperatures thawing the lake, it begged to be used, even just for a night."

Her gaze drifted out over the lake as she snuggled deeper under the blanket. "I love that you went through all this planning—for me."

I lifted her hand up. She turned, staring into my eyes as I gently kissed her knuckles. "I did it for us. For you *and* for me. We've had an amazing year, but it all began on Valentine's Day."

She began to smile. "On a dock, overlooking a lake."

"Yep." My sister's backyard. After we'd both dealt with the heavy emotions of our past, then bared our scars to one another. "I consider it our beginning. When you'd trusted your heart enough to open up to me."

Unshed tears glittered in her eyes as her tiny smile stretched wider. "I love our beginning."

"Me too." I leaned forward and kissed her softly.

We'd forgotten the gondolier. All the world beyond us faded away. Only Hannah and I existed as her soft lips teased mine, nipping and sucking.

When she pulled back, I wrapped my arm around her and something poked my other side. "Oh." I'd been cradling the delicate thing under my coat since the drugstore, waiting for just the right moment. "I have another surprise." On a quick prayer that I hadn't crushed the poor thing, I whipped out one of my secret purchases between us.

Long stemmed, and apparently durable, the pure white rose looked no worse for wear. Its large bud had just begun to open.

"Wow. It's beautiful." With care, she slid her fingers over the outer petals, then angled the flower toward her. She lowered her nose to it and inhaled deeply, her eyes drifting shut.

When she opened them, amusement glittered there. "You bought all the red roses in Manhattan. But only give me a single white one?"

"One white rose." I kissed her softly. "I Googled it. It signifies innocence, peace. White roses are for beginnings."

She took it from me, cupping it by the base of the opening flower. "It's perfect."

"You're perfect," I whispered, my lips trailing down her neck until she shivered.

On a contented sigh, I relaxed back with my arm around her. I pulled the blanket up, tucking her in to keep her warm.

Then we just sat and took in the scenery: the dark shapes of the trees surrounded the lake, the glittering lights of The Loeb Boathouse along the far shore.

"Are you feeling more at peace now?" she asked, her tone soft.

I blinked, surprised at her question. Hadn't thought a thing about my haunting dreams since dinner. "Yeah. I am, actually."

"Good." She gave a hard nod. "I think you just needed to let it go. Realize more important things in your life are worth embracing."

I pulled the champagne bottle from the bucket, then

unwrapped the wire and foil from the top. "That was the whole reason for this trip. I wanted to make the weekend amazing. To make new memories for Valentine's Day."

While holding the bottle in my right hand, I gripped the cork and twisted the base. The cork gave way with a loud *pop!* and I tilted the neck toward the water as some foam surged out.

I poured Champagne into each of the flutes. Then I handed one to her. "To new beginnings."

Her lips curved into a smile as she clinked her glass with mine. "To new beginnings." She took a sip, then stared ahead as the gondola quietly glided through the water.

Spreading my arm wide out before us, I tilted my head toward her. "To gondola rides in Central Park."

She glanced at me. "To romantic dinners where we seize what's important in life."

"To hitting black ice and getting stuck in a snowbank." I shrugged.

She stared up into the sky, then dropped her gaze down to me, the corners of her lips twitching. "To riding my man while stuck in a snowbank."

"*Fuck*," I whispered. "I'll drink to that."

We clinked glasses again, and she took another sip.

The black backdrop of trees ahead seemed to glimmer. The night air had a crisp feel to it, a mineral tang hanging heavy around us. I focused more closely on the grove of trees until I made out the tiny shapes drifting down.

Hannah sat up straighter. "It's snowing!"

Sure as hell was. In the middle of our holiday, the weather granted us one more favor.

Hannah stuck out her tongue, trying to catch the falling snowflakes.

I sighed, happy as fuck. "Damn, I love you."

She beamed one of those megawatt smiles at me. "I love you, Kincade Joseph Michaelson."

"Oh, full names now? Sounds serious."

She turned, fully facing me. "Oh, I am serious."

I glanced at her nearly full glass. "Don't like the Champagne?" I'd ordered the very best.

Lifting her glass near my almost empty one, she gave me a hard stare. "To peeing in cups."

I burst out laughing. "That's some toast you got there. And I thought that subject was taboo, never to be spoken of."

She leaned forward, whispering conspiratorially, "It goes with my next toast."

"Oh. Well, in that case..." I poured more Champagne into my glass and topped hers off.

I waited.

She took a deep breath.

"To peeing on sticks," she blurted out.

I narrowed my eyes, lowering my glass. "Wait...what?"

Her expression flickered, her smile fading. She blew out a slow breath through pursed lips. After a deep inhale, she took my hand. "Happy Valentine's Day...Daddy."

I blinked hard. "Daddy? Me?" Yeah. Great words. But guys got dumb when struck with shocking news like that.

Her apprehensive smile tethered me to reality. "It's good news, right?"

"It's the best news." Without hesitation, I tugged her into my arms.

She pulled back, then gave me a tender kiss. "You wanted a big weekend. Looks like we ended it with a fireworks finale. Does this memory work for you?"

A cramp choked the base of my throat, and I nodded. As a guy who thought he controlled it all, I shot zero to sixty, overcome with emotion. I wrapped my arms around her and kissed her with all the passion I felt for her.

Because no matter how hard I tried, no matter what curveballs life spun our way, incredible miracles happened in the middle of it all.

And Hannah delivered—would be delivering—the most amazing one of all.

EPILOGUE
A NEW ERA

As it turned out, running a specialty bar at the edge of Fairmount Park ended up being easier than we'd thought. With experience from Loading Zone, and a fast education from the sommelier we'd hired, our inventory carried only the finest wines. At his guidance, we offered well-known varietals and smaller boutique names, with by-the-glass prices hitting all ends of the scale.

Hannah stood to the far end of the room, talking with a trio of guests by the patio. They all laughed at something she said.

And she'd never looked more incredible. Her face was a little rounder, cheeks pinked. Her belly was *far* rounder, like she'd stuffed a watermelon up under her sundress.

She was due in a few weeks, mid-September. We calculated back that he was conceived over our honeymoon.

Yep. You heard right. The baby's a "he" with enormous ultrasound balls to prove it.

This was our baby shower. A "couples" shower: Kristen had insisted. With Hannah wanting everyone to be here, we unanimously approved Kristen's idea. The room was filled with decorations of silver and baby blue. The centerpiece flowers were a pale yellow. The table along the side wall held a mountain of presents, half of which had been opened after the crowd had chanted, "*Presents, presents...*" But midway through unwrapping, Hannah had to pee. And she hadn't quite made it back over.

I pulled out my phone and shot her a text.

Miss me? You look amazing . . .

She reached into the front pocket of her dress, glanced down, then smiled.

Her immediate reply popped up.

. . .

I grinned. Didn't need anything more. Our inside joke, those three naughty little dots, did more in one instant to warm our hearts than any other thing we could send.

By the time I worked my way across the room, Hannah had joined both Kristen, the one who'd orchestrated this shindig, and her husband, Jason. Kristen broke free from Jason's arms and wasted no time in putting her hands on either side of Hannah's belly before placing a kiss in the center–like everyone in my family did.

Hannah didn't mind the touchy-feely, and neither did I. She'd been pulled into the fold as if she'd always been one of our own. And Hannah thrived on all the love and attention. Besides, a monumental event was about to take place, ushering a very important person into the world—the first Michaelson baby of the next generation.

As if a family all-call had been sounded, the rest of the

Michaelson Clan began to migrate from their scattered positions in the large dining room and patio, congregating around the guest of honor.

"Hey, babe." I slid an arm around her shoulder.

"Hey there, my sexy man." She beamed me a smile and kissed me softly.

The next thing I knew, Kiki and Kendall edged me out of the way, wrapping Hannah into a gentle hug from either side. I shook my head, laughing.

Ben and Mase descended, politely guiding my sisters out of the way, then giving Hannah a group guy hug.

Hannah squealed at their arrival. "Boys!" She immediately tugged them over to the cake table and began serving them each up a slice from their favorite flavor: cream cheese frosted chocolate bacon. She'd left that green-colored alphabet block untouched, just for them. The rest of the nursery toyland cake had already been systematically destroyed, as any good play room should be. Everyone had devoured their favorite flavored sections: red velvet, carrot cake, pumpkin spice, and chocolate pecan. The glittering blue rocking horse still remained intact, but the train set was missing half the cars, and Mr. Potato Head had seen better days.

Hannah's father, Paul, and his wife, Melanie, stepped in by my side. Paul shook my hand and gave me a half hug. "You've done well."

"Thanks." Praise from a man who'd been involuntarily absent from Hannah's life, but worked to reclaim the family he'd lost, came high in my book.

"With the restaurant *and* my daughter," he clarified.

I nodded toward Hannah. "The restaurant had as much to do with Hannah as me. But your daughter and our son mean more to me than anything in this world."

Paul grinned. "I might've missed out on Hannah's childhood, but I experienced fatherhood with my twins. No other thing will be more satisfying."

Melanie leaned in, shifting her large glass of red wine to her other hand. "Or exhausting."

Mom rushed over with Dad in tow. She moved in beside Hannah, a bright smile on her face. "Have you *seen* this outfit?" She held up the tiniest piece of white fabric by its short sleeves, over which blue suspenders were attached to blue-and-green plaid shorts. A matching plaid Gatsby cap dangled from her fingers. "It's precious."

Dad glanced at Mom as he shoved his hands into his pockets. Happiness shone in his eyes. Then he raised his gaze to me. He gave me a nod, his expression hardening, fierce with pride.

I gave him a head tilt, then grinned wide.

Couldn't help it. I was the happiest fucker of them all.

SEVERAL HOURS LATER, we relaxed in the quiet of our home. We'd chosen the small cottage Hannah had grown up in as our first place we'd live. My house hadn't been set up for a family. But her cozy home held some of our best memories and was perfect. Until our growing family would require us to find or build a new one.

By the soft glow from beneath the Classic Pooh lampshade, we stood in the room our baby would occupy, Hannah nestled into my hold, leaning back against my chest. She trailed her fingers over the top rail of the maple crib. Then her gaze drifted up to the collected hanging artwork, soft watercolors of Pooh and his friends on adventures. I'd surprised her with the four framed illustrations earlier this morning as her baby shower gift from me.

I shifted my hands to the sides of her beautiful belly, then leaned sideways and kissed her temple. "Whatcha thinkin' about?"

She glanced up at me, a radiant smile on her face. "How perfect is this?"

I dropped my head, whispering into her ear. "You're perfect."

Never in a million years would I have imagined feeling like I might explode with this much happiness—certainly not before Invitation Only had brought Hannah into my life.

What tempered all of the sappy feel-good? Worry. My protective instincts had kicked into overdrive: about making sure Hannah had every single thing she needed, that we were ready for the baby, that I'd done everything possible to ensure they were both safe.

The nightmares? Gone.

In fact, the moment I'd gotten the life-altering news on a gondola ride in middle of Central Park, my entire world had shifted on its axis—in the best kind of way. Things I'd once worried about? Inconsequential.

At the beginning, I'd had a recurring dream where Hannah's water had broken, I'd raced her to the hospital, and we'd had our baby boy to take home. Only there were no baby clothes to put him in, no car seat to keep him safe, and when I'd rushed down to the car, only my motorcycle sat in the parking space. Every time the alarming dream happened, I bolted out of bed, hurried into the front room, and took inventory, yet again, making certain we'd bought all the clothes and the car seat.

But those disturbing dreams came less and less often. Hannah had been right all along. Nightmares were unsettling, but their power faded the more we accepted our fears and embraced the wonderful things in our reality.

She shifted in my arms, bringing me back into the amazing present moment.

Then she suddenly crooked her head, nodding toward the wall. "Why aren't there any of Pooh with his honey pot?"

I shot her a deadpan look. "He's *so* not ready for honey."

———

Thank You!

Thank you for experiencing Cade and Hannah's romantic adventure with us in *For Valentine's*.

If you enjoyed the story, please express your love for *For Valentine's* by recommending it to friends in person, by email, on Goodreads, and through book clubs and reader groups.

And if you value reviews to help guide you into your next book, as we do, please help other readers by sharing your review of *For Valentine's* on your favorite retailer and book community sites.

Incredible thanks to everyone for extending your love of *For Valentine's*.

———

Reviews are cherished love notes to authors
and tantalizing invitations to readers.
Appreciated by all. ♥

Want to Read More?

Dive into the steamy romantic comedy of the
No Weddings Series...
No Weddings
One Funeral
Two Bar Mitzvahs
Three Christmases
For Valentine's

Read more of your favorite characters from the No
Weddings series in the steamy spinoff
Unbreakable Series...

Kiki & Darren's romance ignites in...
Heartbreaker

Mase & Leilani's passion flares in...
Rule Breaker

Ben & Shay flirt with danger in...
Lawbreaker

Escape into award-winning time travel romance
in the steamy novels of the
Highland Legends Series...
Forged in Dreams and Magick
Bound by Wish and Mistletoe
Born of Mist and Legend
Found in Flame and Moonlight

———

Adventure in paranormal short stories
in a spinoff of Highland Legends
THE TRAVELER: Initiate Years ...
Veil of Realms
Secrets of Alexandria
Panther Rising
Stones of Power
Highland Magick

———

Want to Read EVEN More?

Icebreaker and *Ball Breaker*
AND
an epic romantasy series are all coming soon!

Be the first to receive preorder alerts, exclusive bonus gifts,
and occasional free stories...
Join our Bastion Family Adventurers!
katbastion.com/email-subscription

ALSO BY KAT & STONE BASTION

No Weddings Series

No Weddings · One Funeral

Two Bar Mitzvahs · Three Christmases

For Valentine's

Unbreakable Series

Heartbreaker · Rule Breaker · Lawbreaker

Forthcoming: *Ball Breaker · Icebreaker*

Highland Legends Series

Forged in Dreams and Magick

Bound by Wish and Mistletoe

Born of Mist and Legend

Found in Flame and Moonlight

THE TRAVELER: Initiate Years

Veil of Realms · Secrets of Alexandria · Panther Rising

Stones of Power · Highland Magick

Half-Baked Holidays

Half-baked Holidays:

A Romantic Comedy Holiday Collection

Heartbreaker

Kiki...

For a blessed few hours, I forgot.

Loading Zone did that to me. The nightclub's Industrial Grunge feel, which I'd helped design with its exposed brick and rusted steel, wrapped itself around me like a comfortable blanket. Heavy bass thumped, vibrating into my bones. My thighs burned from dancing back-to-back songs. Three lemon drop martinis in the last two hours hummed warmth through my veins.

"C'mon," my sister Kendall shouted above the loud music as she grasped my hand, then tugged me forward. "My toes are numb."

Out of breath, I nodded and we headed toward the corner booth the eight of us had crammed into earlier. I dance-walked in the narrow path through the crowd behind her, each step a hip shake and head toss to the pulsing rhythm.

The moment we reached the table, our oldest sister, Kristen, pulled her husband from the booth. "Time for us to go. Jason has an early flight tomorrow."

Cade, our brother and silent partner of Loading Zone, guided his new wife, Hannah, out right after them. "Last dance, Mrs. Michaelson?"

Which left Cade's two best friends: the scruffy prodigy surfer Mase, his former roommate; and clean-cut businessman Ben, the other owner of Loading Zone. I slid over the black distressed leather before landing in the center of the wide, shallow booth to face the dance floor while Mase abandoned his spot on the opposite side to anchor the end next to me.

I grasped the stem of my martini glass, sipped the last bit of the tart lemon drop, then let out a happy-buzz sigh. Being around these three—including rising-star architect Kendall —all of them with their shit together, lent some grounding *yin* to my artistic *yang*.

"Sex on a stick, twelve o'clock," Kendall announced.

My heart suddenly slammed into my ribs. But I exhaled slowly, trying to hide my reaction.

I'd been excited about tonight for several reasons: banish my secret problems from my head, surround myself with my favorite peeps, and *Darren Cole*.

Ben snorted out laughter while Mase dropped me a deadpan look. "'Sex on a *stick*'?"

I shot Mase a sidelong glare and elbowed him in the ribs.

He grunted and nudged my arm away.

By the time I glanced up, corded forearms shot over the outer edge of the table. Large hands planted with a hard smack on the brushed metal tabletop. A familiar folded strip of paper skittered out from his fingers, sliding in a wide arc toward Ben.

My breath caught as I stared into Darren's dark green eyes. A lock of his shaggy black hair fell over his forehead as he tilted his face downward. He set his jaw, expression hardening, as a scuffle between four guys unfolded right behind him, the apparent cause of his sudden hand-plant. He gave me a piercing look. "Twenty minutes."

Then he turned and grasped the nearest offender by the scruff of his shirt. Security arrived an instant later and manhandled the others into submission.

As Darren flexed his left arm while leading his guy toward the exit of the club, the tapered point of a tribal tattoo peeked out from the back collar of Darren's black T-shirt. My imagination began to paint what lay hidden from view: thick black ink arcing across sculpted back muscles, a woven design that twisted downward toward his tight...

"What's that?" Kendall leaned over the table.

I tore my gaze away from Darren and reached for the note, but Kendall snatched up the slip of paper first. She unfolded it and read its message aloud, "'*Gimme a* ride? *K.*'"

"Oh, sure." Mase took a long pull from his beer, then swallowed. "Kendall gets to innuendo the fuck out of this, but I don't?"

Ben arched a brow. "Twenty minutes. That's one helluva ride."

"Shut up. Both of you. Guys objectify women. We can do the same. And it's a ride home, smartass." I tried to shoot Ben an annoyed glare, but the corners of my mouth twitched into a smile and ruined the whole thing.

"*Suuure*...a ride home." Mase winked at me, then glanced over to where Darren strode along the edge of the room as he headed back toward his DJ booth. "I suppose he qualifies."

"Worthy of objectifying? Darren more than qualifies." I pinched the message *meant for Darren's eyes only* and ripped it from Kendall's grasp. "He doesn't say much," I continued. "Leaves the club with different women. Built like the perfect male specimen..."

Ben choked on his beer. "And what are we? Male rejects?"

"Ewww." Kendall scowled. "That's incestuous."

"You're like our brothers. Can't even..." I scrunched my nose and blanked out my mind, willing myself not to visualize it.

"Not looking for love?" Ben asked, tone softening.

At that, all of our gazes drifted toward the dance floor. One of the last songs of the night streamed a fast tempo from the speakers, but in the center of a thinning crowd, Cade and Hannah stood oblivious. Wrapped together, they swayed to a slow rhythm only they seemed to hear. The look of adoration on their faces as they stared deep into each other's eyes spoke volumes.

"No," I said with absolute conviction. "Heartache lies down that road."

Mase laid a gentle hand on mine. "As your pseudo-brother, I'm warning you: Be careful."

I had no idea whether he meant Darren specifically or men in general. It didn't really matter. I'd learned my love lesson early. And I'd never trusted a guy enough to let one hurt me since.

Darren? The only kind of guy I was willing to play with. A beautiful man I refused to form any attachment to—easy to leave.

The quintessential heartbreaker.

In Darren's truck. Again. A vast awkward distance between us. *Again.*

The drive took only about ten minutes. But the ride home from Loading Zone in Philly's Old City Arts District to the outskirts of sleepy Glenhaven—the third since last summer—stretched eternal.

Why? A hookup shouldn't be this difficult.

My gaze shifted toward him. Powerful hands gripped the steering wheel, thumbs knocking some unheard drumbeat into the silence of the cab. Sculpted forearms stretched up toward cut biceps that vanished under the thin black fabric of the T-shirt that hugged them. His expression was serious, but relaxed. As if he didn't feel the weight of the moment like I did.

Now or never, Kiki.

I took a deep breath and ran a flattened hand over the gauzy material of my skirt, trying to calm myself. Then I inched closer to him, needing some sort of validation that whatever tenuous thing we had between us was moving toward something...fun...instead of away from it.

Tonight didn't have to be a big deal. He either wanted me or didn't. Two other platonic drop-offs didn't mean anything significant. Maybe he was shy. Or a gentleman.

As we drove, yellow pools of light from wrought iron lampposts marked the passing time in a visual cadence. *Light...dark. Light...dark.* The streetlights soon began to feel like a countdown, as if they mocked me for just sitting passively in their spotlights.

Yet how to breach the uncomfortable silence? My mind tumbled over the possibilities: *How did your sound board glide tonight? Wow, how 'bout the heavy bass on that last song?*

He cleared his throat, beating me to it. "Sooo...talk to me. How's the art going?"

"Good." *Good? Really?* I winced at my pathetic attempt at conversation.

We made the second-to-last turn, my time running out, as he gave a single nod in reply.

Buck up, Kiki. You either want him or you don't. Stop being a pussy. "Actually, it's a smaller sculpture. A single orchid sprouting from a rocky riverbed."

He glanced my way. "You work with metal, right?"

"Yeah." I leaned back, staring out the windshield, finally calming a bit as I thought about my art. "This piece is bronze. The lone color is the violet on the flower."

"Sounds cool." His voice lowered. He cleared his throat again.

Had he moved closer?

Impossible. He was driving. Behind the steering wheel, as always.

Yet our legs nearly touched. The rough denim, tight over his thigh, had slid over the tan leather seat to within an inch of my bared knee; he'd spread his legs wider.

The man already consumed most of the space in the truck with his commanding presence. But instead of moving away, I automatically drew closer. My thundering pulse throbbed heavier, warmer...lower.

I swallowed hard, attempting to find my way back to the conversation. "How did your night go?" Maybe his sound board was a medium for his art, like metal was for me.

"Good." The corner of his mouth twitched into a barely perceptible grin, then relaxed.

He dropped his right hand from the steering wheel and floated it in the infinitesimal space between us. Gentle pressure rubbed through the flimsy fabric that covered my upper thigh.

My gaze lowered from the dashboard at the exact moment the knuckle of his index finger trailed in slow motion up the skin under my hem.

I held my breath.

I haven't been imagining things.

But then his hand suddenly lifted and fisted. His expression hardened as he stared straight ahead. We made the final turn onto my street, and he eased off the gas, letting us coast. The ride I'd been waiting all night for—six long months and two failed attempts for—appeared to be over.

We rolled to a stop in front of the white picket fence that surrounded the darling butter-yellow Victorian. Then he shifted the truck into park, letting it idle.

Refusing to give up, especially when I sensed him struggling with an attraction we both knew was real, I made a final direct attempt. "You don't have to drive right off. You could come in for a drink."

"No, I can't."

"Why not?" The two words tripped out flippant in my pitiful effort to sound nonchalant.

"You're Cade's little sister."

"No, I'm n—" I blinked.

The pad of his finger pressed to my lips. Warm. Firm. Suddenly, I thought of nothing else. My whole world became our tantalizing first contact.

He didn't move. Simply stared at me.

I closed my eyes. My head eased back against the headrest, but the contact remained as my lips pursed into the gentlest kiss against his fingertip. I wanted to flick my tongue out, taste him. But then he pulled away.

I blinked my eyes open.

He'd half-twisted on the seat toward me. "You deserve better than a one-night fuck, Kiki."

"What I deserve," I muttered, then snorted.

Damn right, I deserve better than that.

But one night was all I could handle.

"Doesn't matter." What I continued to tell myself. "What

I want right now is you." There, I'd said it. Out in the open. Bold and direct.

"What you deserve *does* matter. Don't ever forget it." His voice hardened with every word. His dark brows furrowed to the point a deep crease marred the tanned skin between them.

Without thinking, I reached up and pressed my thumb along that vertical line, massaging until his face began to relax.

He stared at me with renewed intensity. "What are you doing?"

"Trying to get you to chill out." I let my thumb slide a fraction to the right until I found a pressure point, then I spread the rest of my fingertips across the line of his eyebrow. "Is it working?"

"No." The corners of his mouth twitched again.

"Liar."

"Okay. A little."

"Seriously, though," I continued as if I hadn't been distracted by his impressive scowl. "I'm an excellent one-night fuck."

He jerked his head away, then lapsed into a coughing fit.

I arched a brow. "What? Don't think so?"

He shook his head. "No." His mouth fell open. "I mean, I'm sure you are." He blew out a heavy sigh, cheeks puffing from the effort. "You just..."

"Unnerve you?"

"*Yes*." He thrust a splayed hand into the open air between us with the curt word. "Are you trying to kill me?"

A smile began to curve my lips. "No, I'm just trying to—"

"Don't say it."

The word hung on the tip of my tongue. "You know I'm thinking it."

"Stop thinking it." He took a measured breath, his chest gradually rising, then falling.

Enjoying the loaded tension between us, I remained still, waiting.

When he turned toward me again, I leaned closer and deeply inhaled his earthy scent. "Look. This doesn't have to be complicated just because I'm Cade's sister. You're an adult. I'm an adult. Aren't you attracted to me?"

Every telltale sign he'd shown suggested that he wanted me. But I'd never encountered so much resistance in a guy before. Then again, I'd never had one in my sights so long before either. I ignored the implications in that.

"Of course I am." He draped an arm along the top of the seatback.

His warmth lured me in, and I edged even closer until my entire side crushed against his. He made no move to stop me and didn't flinch away, but his lengthy pause indicated that he resisted committing to anything.

"All it has to be is one night," I whispered, my lips nearly touching the warm skin of his neck.

Another heavy sigh ruffled the hair above my ear, shooting chill bumps down my side. "You gotta know, if I could...I would. It *is* complicated. I can't explain. But no matter how badly either of us want to, this can't happen."

I blinked, confused and lost in uncharted territory. Never had a guy not taken the bait I'd offered. And he was being so nice about it. My mind couldn't process what was happening. "You want me."

"Fuck, yes. I mean, no." He growled in frustration. "Goddammit, Kiki. Just get out of the truck. Please."

I pulled away from him and straightened in my seat, almost laughing at the desperation in his tone. Then I dared a glance at him. His expression grew tortured. A tiny part of me felt bad for putting him in a position I didn't understand. The rest of me beamed that I wasn't the only sexually frustrated one in the vehicle.

Not yet willing to admit defeat, I gave him a smile and grasped the cold metal door handle. "Thanks for the ride, Darren."

I wouldn't ask for one again. But I didn't need to. The seeds had been planted. My work was done. Either he wanted me enough to get past whatever obstacle was cockblocking his way, or he didn't.

Meanwhile, I'd go back to the life I'd been trying to forget, once my mind-numbing buzz wore off.

I wanted to glance over my shoulder as I unfastened the painted wooden gate, double-check to see if he was still watching, but I fought the urge.

The low hum of his idling truck engine remained unchanged. But had his mind?

This lonely girl can only hope.

Enjoy the rest of the romance...
Heartbreaker

Found in Flame and Moonlight

Eight minutes was all Chelsea Smith had. All she needed. *Hopefully.*

The heavy wooden door to Professor MacLaren's private office snicked closed behind her. With a subtle suggestion from her mind, the tumblers reengaged within its lock, a deadbolt she'd "picked" with similar mental ease mere seconds ago.

On her next inhale of cooler undisturbed air, the distinctive scents of age washed over her: that certain spice of centuries-old leather, a mustiness of layered dust, the sweetness of yellowing paper in a prized collection of ancient books.

The room's furnishings echoed its owner's passion for antiquities. Within a sizable entry, a vintage coffee-colored Chesterfield sofa with matching wingchairs hovered at the edge of a burgundy-and-gold Aubusson carpet. Along the side and far wall, relics from exotic locales perched from various niches between precisely stacked scholarly tomes in massive bookcases. And beyond a sizable polished wood desk and its stately leather chair, within tall display cases that flanked a large window, treasured discoveries from historic digs rested on glass shelves.

Yet one particular artifact stood apart from the rest. The

sole reason for her break-in. And the item occupied the nearest corner of his polished wood desk, exposed. No bookcase niche. No protective case.

"Such unfathomable *power*," Chelsea murmured toward the rectangular object, at once fascinated and intrigued. More than she'd been about anything in her first twenty-two years of an immortal life hiding-in-plain sight among "normal" humans.

Her excitement even eclipsed what she'd witnessed from the other side of that window while walking to MacLaren's lecture less than an hour ago.

Though her mind still reeled about that discovery as well.

Because something very *not human* had stood near that power-drenched box, partially transparent, as if not fully materialized into the human world. And that shirtless muscular something had resembled artistic depictions of male angelic warriors, only skewed darker and more sinister with its dusky olive skin, inky black wings, and blue-green prismatic eyes.

And the enigmatic creature had stared directly at her, eyes narrowing, puzzlement twisting his sharp features as Chelsea blatantly stared back. He'd seemed surprised. That she could detect him? Or perhaps that their paths had intersected in the first place.

Yet inside the professor's locked office, no sign of the dark angel remained.

Seven minutes.

The forceful vibration of the artifact's unique power was what had caught her attention from the other side of the window. It had radiated an exhilarating and complex energy, beckoning her like a siren's call.

"Invitation accepted," she whispered.

With slow breaths, Chelsea banked her excitement. Not hard to achieve. Her kind, further evolved humans, born-and-bred assassins, had been trained through millennia to suppress emotion.

"Yeah." She let out a soft snort. "Look how well *that* turned out."

Members of her race had recently evolved again. And an underground faction had organically formed. One that no longer sought to squelch their emotions. That strong minority yearned for something greater, a deeper meaning to their eternal life.

Months ago, Chelsea had been secretly contacted by them. The founders had detected her tendency to operate on the fringe of acceptability. Of course, she'd joined their cause without hesitation.

In the hours and days following that pivotal decision, she'd eased the cognitive restraints that had hobbled her. They had warned her that she would suffer unimaginable internal struggle. Yet nothing had prepared her for the cascade of emotions. One in particular had caused an enormous dissonance with her inherited vocation.

Empathy had bled into her black-and-white world.

An *assassin's* world.

And that problematic emotion had caused a thunderstorm of chaotic gray.

Six minutes.

Focus, Chelsea. She took measured steps toward the charged artifact, noting its unusual features. A foot long, half that wide and tall, a rectangular box sat encased in layers of elaborate metallic latticework. The gleaming designs that adorned its corners and edges were comprised of various metals from differing artistry. But beneath those ornate motifs, simpler flat sides were fashioned from a beautiful bluish-silver metal with a slight sparkle to its sheen.

Indirect bright light glowed in from the large window, but as Chelsea approached, an aura of energy haloed around the box. Infinitesimal particles glittered beyond its surfaces, flashes of silver and gold visible to her preternatural eyes.

Five minutes.

Which meant MacLaren's lecture in his beloved Advanced Theories in Archaeology had concluded. Earlier, Chelsea had obediently endured the graduate-level course with fifteen other classmates until she'd politely excused herself at the last and most opportune moment. A correct amount of respectful time from a valued student. The perfect window of plausible deniability should her burglary plans go awry.

Students typically waylaid him after his lectures, but to be certain, she extended her superhuman hearing. Down a wide sidewalk between buildings, across a grassy quad, and into the cozy window-lined room that the tenured professor claimed as his own, she detected the voices of eager students who had indeed detained him. Which enabled him to wax eloquent about the week's series and his latest obsession: prehistoric artifacts handed down by gods, breadcrumbs to the secrets of mysterious civilizations.

"But you've been keeping the biggest secret of all right here in your office, haven't you?" Chelsea murmured as she paused within reach of the object.

Four minutes.

Plenty of time to abort, to walk away without detection.

"I don't *need* to be here." Sound reason.

And yet, need had become relative.

For in the months following her recent evolution, an

undefinable hunger had begun to grow that nothing satisfied. A craving for a deeper purpose. Not the deadly one mandated by her ancestry. Not even the glimmer of hope that her emerging faction offered.

"Something personal," she murmured, staring at the box. She'd been hunting a cause that matched her sudden passion for life. Unique and special. Sparked by her newfound awakening. "Worthy. And all my own."

Because every action she'd taken in life, from actual missions to basic periphery cover, had been by her race's directive. Even attending university. Particularly MacLaren's courses.

But for the first time, she operated on her own volition. Because before that morning, she hadn't been privy to any details of *why* MacLaren had become a person of interest. Until one shining detail had made itself known, flashing its undeniable energy straight toward her.

Therefore, the risk of exposure? While investigating an object as exceptional as what she hoped to discover about herself?

More than acceptable.

While she continued to listen, the distinct voices of six fellow grad students dwindled to two hardcore disciples. They peppered the professor with questions, theories, and offers of assistance on his next expedition. Groveling, as usual. But MacLaren had their number. And only a couple of minutes remained of his scheduled patience.

Chelsea drew a deep breath to calm her riotous—clearly *not* suppressed—emotions.

Instinct screamed the intricate box held her destiny. Even if she had no idea why.

But as she took a final step and reached out a hand to touch, its unique power reacted to her proximity with accelerating vibrations of energy—plenty of evidence to back up that gut feeling.

Three minutes.

MacLaren shooed out his fan club with his parting excuses and locked up the classroom.

Right as Chelsea hovered a hand over the artifact.

Energy emanated upward from that bluish-silver top, charging the air with electrons that sizzled and sparked. Warmth bathed her palm. Friendly. Inviting. *Intoxicating.*

Until a sense of grave danger spiked in those scant inches between the mysterious metal and her skin. And an unfamiliar feeling of trepidation tripped down her spine. Like some cosmic warning.

Chelsea paused, then blinked heavily, thrown by the sudden unfriendliness of the box and her own emotion about it. She wiggled her fingers within the box's charged aura and considered her impulsive actions. And their unknown ramifications. With the artifact. And MacLaren.

An extensive list of potentialities scrolled through her advanced mind. But the calculations magnified when she removed the laws of the known universe and input alternate realities. Involving energized boxes. And dark angels. And supposedly regular professors that capture the attention of a race of assassins.

Ninety seconds.

"So many possibilities," she murmured about the upside. *Too many variables to calculate.*

Chelsea snorted and shook her head with a slight smile. "I've never been afraid of anything in my life." Headlong into the adventure. The only way she saw the world.

The leather heels of MacLaren's loafers clicked down the nearest sidewalk.

Less than a minute. Before her trespass was discovered.

Urgency fired through her veins. She tensed her arm and lowered her hand, ready to touch no matter the outcome. To finally complete some circuit she'd begun to sense, as if the dark matter hovering between the spaces in the universe needed her help.

The charged air rippled with a stronger dose of caution.

Chelsea narrowed her eyes at the box.

Are you trying to communicate with me?

That the inanimate object had sentience, as opposed to some other force out in the ether, gave her pause. Deadly animals and insects often displayed vivid warnings of their lethal venom.

But why lead me here with such clear invitation? Do you not want me to touch?

The warning vibration wavered back and forth in response as the additional questions crossed her mind. Not quite a yes, not quite a no. That it wanted her there, perhaps. But not to touch? *Orrr...*

"Not yet?" Barely an inch existed.

A hot glow sparkled into existence between her and the artifact, golden and shimmering. The box's energy extended an exquisite representation of agreement in its special language.

"Fascinating." Mesmerizing.

The artifact's seductive power continued to astound.

Have you taunted MacLaren with such scandalous invitation?

No sooner had she posed the mental question, than an answer rippled forth. Only that message vibrated not from the artifact, but from somewhere out in the ether. *No.* Crystal clear. Not as any legible word, but a negative in resonance.

The energized box did not wait on that desk for the professor.

At that moment, the artifact existed for a singular purpose: to join its immense power with hers.

MacLaren's footfalls began to click down the tiles of the building's corridor.

Energy spiked from the box again. Even while its power rippled another caution: *Not yet.* The message clearly vibrated from the object, not the ether.

But unraveling the mysteries of a higher consciousnesses in matter and space had to wait.

Adrenaline surged through her. "Out of time."

Golden sparks fountained up from its metallic top, singeing her palm. *Not yet!*

"When?" Chelsea choked out a laugh at the box. "*After he has campus security cuff me?*"

MacLaren's key slid into the lock.

Her pulse raced, the thump of her heart a drumbeat in her ears.

Now or never! she argued to the unseen gatekeepers.

Tiny clicks echoed as tumblers released in the lock's mechanism.

The door edge scraped over its frame, the only means of a clean escape swinging open and her window of opportunity closing right along with it.

Half-assed alibies spun through her mind, all utterly ridiculous: *I followed a burglar in, I needed to lie down and only your pin-tucked sofa would do, I saw a black-winged angel with sparkling blue-green eyes staring out your window.* Voicing that last factoid? Bordered on certifiable insanity.

But at the last split second between clean infiltration and utter discovery—right as her anxiety skyrocketed—a powerful vacuum slammed her hand down that remaining inch.

A scorching current charged up through her palm from the metal. Blinding power and incredible pleasure flashed through her being.

MacLaren's office vanished.

And a realm of absolute nothingness descended.

———

Gawain Brodie sucked in a stunned breath as the inside of his chest...*boomed*.

Thunder? Confused, he frowned but refused to break stride. He raced down an earthen footpath in the shadowy forest to rejoin his warriors; he'd been ambushed while scouting. And since no cloud marred the late-afternoon sky, he shook off the jarring sensation.

Faster! Scant seconds remained. Clan Brodie had been exposed. Their castle's centuries-old secret somehow breached.

Blood from three attackers speckled his arms and chest. Yet the last one's dying words bore evidence of the exposure: *Your magick castle is ours!*

A tang from the skirmish coated his tongue, pungent earth and the coppery taste of blood. Anger churned in his gut. Ferocity pumped through his veins. Single-minded determination overcame burning muscles as he sought to vanquish whatever enemy they faced.

Intent on cutting time, he broke into a sunny glade, ran across rippling purple blooms of heather, then rejoined the well-worn trail. Yet as he rounded the gnarled trunk of an ancient yew, a sudden awareness made him veer wide in the turn.

Alongside the path, lacy fronds of bracken trembled. Then a blur of motion burst forth.

Dark garb registered in his peripheral vision. As did the gleam of a swinging sword.

He unsheathed his own sword, then blocked a strike meant to cleave his neck.

Never pausing his momentum, Gawain twisted his body and shifted forward, swinging his weapon over. Then he tightened his blade down at the last moment for the killing blow.

To his surprise, the swords clashed. Punishing vibration jarred his bones from hand to arm, shoulder to neck, till they rattled a final quiver down through his teeth.

The attacker—a male with flaxen hair, of similar height and breadth to the threesome he'd more easily dispatched —merely sounded a low grunt.

With greater determination, Gawain thrust.

In equal measure, his opponent parried.

Fury darkened his attacker's eyes.

Exhilaration fired through Gawain's veins.

Their deadly battle-dance continued with strikes and blocks, thrusts and parries. Each next metallic crash rang out with echoing menace.

"At long last, a worthy opponent," Gawain murmured.

Gawain arced his sword back around, but once the tip swung skyward, he twisted, tucked, then thrust from a lower angle.

The soldier deflected then stepped aside, just as well trained, equally gifted.

"Aye. An 'opponent' who'll impale yer bloody arse like a stuck pig," the soldier replied in an English accent. A sick hunger gleamed in his eye.

Amused, Gawain relaxed his stance and drew back his weapon. He tilted his head and narrowed his eyes. "Why eat pig when you can dine like a king?"

The man's expression fell. As did the tip of his sword while he gave a heavy blink and furrowed his brow. "What're you on about?"

In the next heartbeat, Gawain lunged with incredible speed. The tip of his sword led the way, piercing the man's heart before he was able to draw a full gasp of surprise—or reengage his sword.

"The differences between us," Gawain whispered into the ear of the dying man.

Severe lack of emotion and abundance of wit.

What Gawain possessed and most did not.

With a quick jerk, Gawain freed his sword. As the body crumpled to the ground, he swiped both sides of his weapon on the cleanest patch of the soldier's woolen tunic. He believed in letting fallen men keep their blood. *Off my sword.*

English! The revelation of how far and wide their exposure had traveled still stunned him.

No time! He charged back toward the footpath and raced on.

After another few hundred yards, the clear sounds of combat filtered into the dense forest: the clatter of weapons, shouts and grunts from men.

Seconds later, he burst upon a greater battle. Or what little remained of it.

His brethren carved and sliced through their own tenacious dark-garbed attackers. One Brodie to five English. But the last of their foe fell in rapid succession, one after the other, none prepared for the skill of the unique clan of Highlanders.

With no immediate threat left to eliminate, Gawain sheathed his weapon.

A second strange thunder boomed through his chest.

And its fading vibration carried the aftertaste of something imminent...*weighty*. As if an event of great import was about to transpire. *Involving me?* Or the clan.

Dismayed by the inexplicable and unnerving sensation, Gawain stared toward the western horizon as a fiery sun dipped below jagged mountain peaks.

Two warhorses suddenly appeared below his line of vision, one snow white, the other coal black. Both materialized seemingly from nowhere. And knowing their riders as Gawain did, they likely had.

Another powerful vibration reverberated through Gawain's chest so hard, he stifled the urge to cough as his family approached.

Astride the white mare was Isobel Brodie with her long blond hair flying back in the wind. Clad in her custom deerskin hunting outfit, she braced her toddler son between her arms.

On the black stallion rode Iain, Isobel's husband, Gawain's older brother, and Laird of Clan Brodie. He cradled their lad's twin sister with a father's protective hand.

Clutched in Iain's other hand was a magickal box whose surface sparkled even in gloaming's waning light.

Yet that box had *never* left Brodie Castle.

Not in all the years of Gawain's life.

Nor in any of the legendary tales of generations past.

An unmistakable sense of foreboding washed over him as his fellow warriors gathered to watch their leader and kin draw near.

"*All* approach the battlefront?" their commander, Robert, inquired to his right.

"With the wee ones?" Duncan asked at his left.

The warriors were part of Iain's elite guardsmen. Twelve in total. Closer than brothers.

"Nay." Naught was as it seemed. A great change had begun. Those facts rang true with every heavy beat of his heart. And he'd somehow landed in the center of its shifting tides. "They'll be but a moment," he murmured.

Even if Gawain failed to comprehend *how* he knew what was about to transpire, he sensed why they'd come.

Fate had descended upon him. Though the circumstance made little sense.

"I'll not take your place!" Gawain objected to the notion. The magickal box may as well have been scepter, orb, and crown. For of the many powers it wielded, foremost among them had long been to ordain the next Brodie male as chieftain of their clan.

"*Aye*, you will." Iain lifted the hallowed box high, reaching back.

"You remain hale and whole." Fit to rule. No reason to shift the obligation.

"We've no time to explain." Isobel tightened her legs to bring her mount alongside Iain's as she glanced at her husband. "Danger abounds. And we've been summoned"—at the last word, she directed Gawain a pointed look, heavy with meaning—"*away*."

Gawain sighed. *Away through* time itself. *No explanation needed.*

A strange feeling quivered in his gut. Akin to uncertainty. And a more familiar one: dread. Of the unknown. Of the burden of a reign he had never expected to shoulder.

The obsessive focus of battle had served him well all his life, had helped him overcome childhood demons. Even to the detriment of relations with close family. Namely his sister, Brigid, who he'd wrongly blamed for the cause of those demons so long ago. But Gawain had already come to accept how he'd done Brigid a grave disservice and labored to make amends.

Of late, he'd grown more noble. Worthy of the reign.

And his brother well knew it.

"'Tis the way of it," Iain bellowed for all the guardsmen to hear in witness of the historic moment. "You'll lead the clan through."

"*Aye.*" Gawain gave a clipped nod to his brother in dutiful acceptance of the role.

Iain dipped his chin with satisfaction, punched his arm forward, and released his grip.

The box arced through the air.

With narrowed eyes, Gawain thrust his hands up to catch it.

Yet at the exact moment his fingertips made contact with its cool metal sides, several monumental events happened at once, in plain sight of their guardsmen.

A bright bolt of lightning shot from ground to sky with a true boom of thunder.

Isobel touched a hand to Iain's shoulder and Clan Brodie's former ruling family vanished, warhorses and all.

Heat sparked from the box to his fingers and flashed through his entire body.

And a raven-haired woman appeared out of thin air. Vibrant blue eyes stared straight at him. Her slender hand rested atop the box.

"*Nay!*" Gawain growled, furious.

In his disgruntled shock of becoming laird, he'd forgotten the *other* burden the ancient box bestowed.

A soul mate.

Enjoy the rest of the adventure...
Found in Flame and Moonlight

ACKNOWLEDGMENTS

Huge thanks to Heather and Misty, our close friends and cheerleaders.

To our social media friends, fans, supporters, readers, reviewers, and bloggers, both those we've interacted with thus far and those we look forward to meeting—we are immensely grateful for all you do. Your unending enthusiasm for reading our stories fuels our excitement to write them.

Stone, what in the world could I say here to cover the depth of my gratitude to you? Not enough. But I will say that I'm so glad we took a wild idea over pizza out one night and turned it into a labor of love and laughter. I'd shout out some of the hilarious moments to make you laugh, but I have a feeling you're already thinking about them...and smiling.

Kat...Wait, what? Is this like wedding vows? You know what you mean to me. The journey. The love. The laughter. *Squirrel!*

ABOUT THE AUTHOR

Kat Bastion won several awards for her bestselling debut novel *Forged in Dreams and Magick*.

Kat & Stone Bastion's bestselling first novel *No Weddings* and the No Weddings series were named Best of 2014 by multiple romance review blogs.

When not defining love and redemption through scribed words, they enjoy hiking in vivid wildflower deserts, ancient tropical forests, and historic urban jungles.

Join our Bastion Family Adventurers!

Be in the know with preorder alerts, exclusive bonus gifts, and occasional free stories:

katbastion.com/email-subscription